Bushwhacked

Maple Syrup Mysteries Book 2

Emily James

Stronghold Books

ONTARIO, CANADA

Emily James
authoremilyjames@gmail.com
www.authoremilyjames.com

This is a work of fiction. I made it up. You are not in my book. I probably don't even know you. If you're confused about the difference between real life and fiction, you might want to call a counselor rather than a lawyer because names, characters, places, and incidents in this book are a product of my twisted imagination. Real locales and public names are sometimes used for atmospheric purposes. Any resemblance to actual people, living or dead, or to businesses, companies, events, and institutions is completely coincidental.

Book Layout ©2013 BookDesignTemplates
Cover Design by Deranged Doctor Designs

Bushwhacked/Emily James. -- 1st ed.
ISBN 978-0-9920372-9-1

For my husband the copy editor, who makes sure I don't write desert when I mean dessert, because no one wants to eat a giant plate of sand.

Every lie is two lies—the lie we tell others and the lie we tell ourselves to justify it.

–ROBERT BRAULT

Chapter 1

If I were a superstitious person, I'd swear some supernatural force wanted to keep me out of Fair Haven. Last time I came into town, a tractor ran me off the road. This time, a January blizzard was trying to do the same.

I leaned closer to my windshield, squinting, and kept my foot lightly on the gas pedal, inching my car forward. My headlights lit up the flakes into a swirling curtain, hiding everything around me. The only indicator that I was even on the road at all was the smoothness of the ground beneath my tires.

Was it safe to stop in the middle of the road during a snowstorm and wait it out, or would someone else come along and run into me? Heavy snow days back home in Virginia meant an unexpected holiday. No one tried to fight their way through it, so I had zero experience with driving in snow. When I set out this morning, I'd checked the weather report for home and they called for clear skies. I'd forgotten how drastically the weather could change the farther north I drove.

I shivered and cranked the heat. I hadn't expected to stay away from Fair Haven for this long. When I left shortly after solving my Uncle Stan's murder, I'd planned to be back within a couple of weeks, well before the heart of winter. But everything took longer than expected, from selling my furniture to subletting my apartment, and by then it was the holidays, and my mom insisted I stay until after Christmas. Given her way, I'd have stayed until spring.

Maybe she'd been right. I was likely going to slide my car off the road and freeze to death out here in the middle of nowhere. The area around Fair Haven was notorious for its cell phone dead zones, so I'd have no guarantee of help if I had an accident, especially this late at night.

My headlights flashed off something blue to the right of the road. The Fair Haven sign? Oh dear Lord, let it be the Fair Haven sign. At least then I'd be inside the town limits and able to walk to a house if I slid off the road.

My car fishtailed, and my heart scrambled up into my throat. I jerked my foot off the gas and clenched my hands around the wheel. The car steadied.

I let out a breath. This was going to be the last time I ever drove in a snowstorm.

I eased my foot back onto the gas, and my car moved forward in a straight line again. The snow lessened slightly, and buildings on either side of the road came into view, more outlines than solid forms, but it was something. Hazy streetlights helped break up the darkness.

The brick in my chest dissolved. I was going to make it.

My car smashed into something, jerking to a halt and sending me forward. The seat belt caught across my chest and yanked me back before my head hit the steering wheel.

I slammed my foot on the brake and threw the car into park. My hands shook. What had I hit? The buildings hunkered down against the storm on either side of me, so I had to still be on the road. Maybe I'd clipped the corner of a white car or truck parked on the side of the street? I wouldn't be able to see a white vehicle in the snow and darkness.

But the impact felt like it came from in front, and I'd swear I felt my wheels try to ride up over something and fail. A deer? Could I have hit a deer? Deer on the road were a common problem in Virginia, but I had no idea how prevalent they were here and in a snowstorm. Hopefully it wasn't a deer. It made me want to cry thinking about an animal suffering.

Maybe I'd just run into a huge snow drift.

I opened my car door and a burst of wind rushed in, sending a shiver coursing over my body. Thankfully the scarf Erik gave me the last time I saw him spared me from snow down my collar.

I picked my way toward the front, running a hand along my car to keep from slipping. It was clear as soon as I neared the tire that I hadn't clipped another vehicle. There wasn't one anywhere nearby. Northerners were probably wise enough not to leave their cars parked on the street during a snowstorm.

I rounded the front bumper and froze. A body lay face-down in the street.

I hadn't hit a deer. I hit a person.

Chapter 2

What had I done? I hadn't even seen him—the short hair and size of the body said it had to be a man. He couldn't be dead, could he? My car wasn't going that fast.

My legs seemed to have iced over and frozen to the ground. Part of me said I should check him, and the other part said I should call 9-1-1 first.

I skidded back to my car and grabbed my purse out of the open door. If he were seriously injured, I wouldn't know where to start to help him. I needed to get an ambulance here as soon as possible.

The screen on my cell phone glowed to life. No signal. I dialed 9-1-1 anyway. The phone beeped in my ear. Useless. I heaved it and my purse back inside the car.

Maybe he was dazed, not unconscious. If he could walk, I could get him into the car and drive him to the hospital. That had to be better than leaving him out in the snow while I went for help.

I ran back to the front of my car and half fell, half knelt beside him. He lay face first in the snow. "Sir, can you hear me? Are you okay?"

I touched a hand to the back of his neck. His skin was warm to the touch. That seemed like a good sign. "Sir?"

I didn't dare shake him, and turning him over seemed more dangerous. His back or neck might be injured. Was he even breathing? I pressed my palm to his back, straining to feel any movement. It didn't seem like he was breathing, but perhaps his breaths were too shallow to feel.

My hands shook. I lifted his arm from the snow and pressed two fingers into his wrist. No pulse. But maybe I wouldn't be able to feel one since his arm had been lying in the snow. He wasn't even wearing a coat. I stripped mine off and laid it over top of him.

I couldn't remember the TV show I'd heard it on, but wasn't there some saying about *you weren't dead until you were warm and dead*. The snow might be a good thing. It might protect him and give me time to bring help for him. I'd leave my coat. Cold was one thing. Hypothermia was entirely another.

The snow had lightened a bit more. I squinted against the flakes. The buildings lining the street were businesses, their lights off and signs flipped to closed, but I recognized the fish and chips place, A Salt & Battery. It was only a couple blocks over from the police station and a guaranteed landline to call for medical assistance.

I climbed back into my car and backed up, navigating around the man in the street. I sent out a prayer that I was making the right choice to leave him and that no one else would run him over in the time it took me to bring back help.

I'd started experimenting with prayer after my Uncle Stan died. My parents were agnostic, but Uncle Stan had believed in a higher power. The events of the past few months had shown me clearly that I wanted to be more like him than I was like my parents. Trying the praying thing seemed like an easy way to start, though I'd soon have to decide if I wanted to learn more because it was getting weird calling whoever I was talking to "Uncle Stan's God."

My car slid a couple of times on the way to the police station, but I managed to keep it on the road. I parked out front of the station.

When I pulled on the station door, it didn't budge. A jolt shot through me like I was falling down a flight of stairs. Were the doors locked? Fair Haven had a small police force. Maybe they didn't staff the station in a blizzard. If there wasn't anyone here, I'd have to drive around, trying to get a signal on my phone.

I yanked the door again, and the coating of ice popped, making it suddenly visible. The door flew open.

I stumbled inside and up to the front desk. The man behind it glanced up, and his eyes widened. He probably hadn't expected anyone to stumble through his door at close to midnight in the middle of a snowstorm. The wide eyes, along with his oversized glasses, made him look a bit like an owl.

"How can I help you?" he asked.

"I hit someone with my car over by A Salt & Battery. They need help."

At least that's what I intended to say. My whole body was shaking, and my teeth chattered, making me slur my words a bit and sound like I might be high.

Owl Man scowled at me, and he pointed toward the chairs, already reaching for the radio. "Take a seat," he said to me.

The cold, hard metal of the bench that ran the length of the wall didn't help my shivering. The image of the man's body lying in front of my car kept playing over in my mind. That man was someone's father or brother or son.

I needed to lie down or I was going to pass out.

I stretched out on the bench, trying not to think about how frequently—or, more likely, infrequently—

it was cleaned. It was either the bench or face-planting on the floor.

I had the vague notion that my mind was wandering, but I couldn't seem to bring it back.

Then Owl Man stood over me. I knew he was saying something, but it was nearly impossible to focus. I thought I caught the words *stupid drunk*.

He hauled me up, and my legs tried to buckle underneath me. He supported me down a narrow hallway and unlocked a cell door.

Was he putting me in a cell? Why was he putting me in a cell? The law in Michigan couldn't be that different from the law in Virginia. I hadn't run the man down on purpose, and I'd immediately sought help for him. I hadn't been speeding or drinking. Accidental deaths didn't bring criminal charges.

I wanted to say all that, but my lips felt heavy and thick and disconnected from my brain. Maybe I was dying, too. Maybe the impact had been harder than I thought and I was bleeding internally. News headlines in Fair Haven's mid-week paper would read *Freak Snowstorm Accident Claims Two Lives*.

Owl Man dropped me more roughly than necessary onto the cot, and the world went black.

Chapter 3

Something soft and feathery tickled my cheek. I peeled open one eye. Soft, feathery, and blue. My scarf. I'd worn my scarf to bed?

The events of the night before came back in an avalanche. I wasn't in my bed. I wasn't even in Uncle Stan's house. I squeezed my eyes shut again. By now the man I'd hit would either be recovering in the hospital or lying on a slab in the morgue. I pushed the thought away before it made me want to pass out again.

I opened my eyes and swung my still-booted feet off the bed. The cell around me appeared to be meant for a single person. The cot underneath me butted up against the longer wall, perpendicular to the bars. A toilet hunkered on the opposite side of the room, next to a cracked sink with a bar of white soap. The soap didn't look new.

A shudder traced its way over my shoulders. Boy did I hope my bladder could hold what I drank yesterday until someone came to get me. There wasn't exactly a door on this place. I didn't know yet if someone was in the cell across the way, and who knew if there were cameras monitoring the cells. I certainly didn't want to flash anyone who might have a view of this cell. Avoiding someone in Fair Haven was like trying not to smell the BO of the person sitting next to you on the Metro.

I stood and stretched my arms over my head. My kinks had knots. The motion moved my keys in the pocket of my jeans.

I turned in a quick circle. My purse wasn't with me, but that wasn't exactly strange. I couldn't remember if I even brought it in, and if I had, the officer who put me in the cell last night probably confiscated it. What was odd was that they'd left me with everything else. They should have taken away at least my scarf and shoelaces in case remorse over whatever I'd supposedly done drove me to suicide.

To my memory, I hadn't been officially charged or booked and fingerprinted either. Had any of that happened, I'd be asking for my phone call and contacting my mom. Even though I'd decided to maintain my license to practice law for now, I knew better than to try to represent myself in anything more serious than a traffic ticket.

Keys rattled behind me, and I spun around. The man on the other side of the door was wiry and balding, the remains of his light brown hair creating a horseshoe on his head. He was the same one who was kind to Russ when Russ and I spent an unfortunate few hours in a police interrogation room right before I returned to Virginia.

His name started with a Q. Quinn? No Quincey. Problem was, I didn't know whether that was his first name or his last name. If I really had done something wrong last night, it wouldn't help my case to call an officer by his first name.

He pulled open the door and froze, as if he'd only now looked at me closely enough to recognize me. "Miss. Dawes."

It didn't seem like the right time to correct him that my last name was really Fitzhenry-Dawes. Everyone here knew me as Stan Dawes' niece, and I'd probably end up having to accept being called Nicole Dawes. The hyphenated last name seemed to trip people up. Hopefully my mom and dad would never need to know.

I peeked at his name tag. *Dornbush.* Quincey must be his first name. "Nice to see you again, Officer Dornbush. I wish the circumstances were better this time than last time, but..." I shrugged. Most people only encountered the police under less-than-wonderful circumstances.

His gaze flickered from my scarf and down to my boots. "You're the drunk hit-and-run driver?"

If we were in a cartoon, my eyes would have bulged a hand's width out of their sockets. As it was, I could feel my mouth hanging open. "I'm the what?"

This didn't make any sense. The officer I reported the accident to last night must have misunderstood. I was so upset that I wasn't exactly communicating clearly.

Officer Dornbush held up a hand. "Hold on."

He left my cell without closing the door. Guess he didn't think I was a flight risk. I moved into the open doorway so I could see what was going on. He went to each of the other cells, peering inside.

When he reached the last cell, he shook his head and came back to me. "You're the only one here. Why don't you tell me real quick what happened last night."

I told him everything I could remember. "I woke up here a few minutes before you came."

Officer Dornbush blew out a puff of air. "Sounds like you went into shock. The Interim Chief isn't going to be happy that you ended up down here instead of being checked out by paramedics." He stepped back out of the doorway, gave a little bow of his head, and swept a hand out in front of him in a *ladies first* gesture. "I'll take you to the chief's office, and we'll sort this out."

I knew the way to the chief's office, but I suppose he couldn't allow me to wander around the station unattended even if he didn't believe I was a criminal.

I hung back to walk beside him. I had one question that wouldn't wait. "You didn't say if the man I hit last night made it."

"I was hoping you wouldn't ask." He avoided eye contact. "I didn't want to have to be the one to tell you we were too late to save him."

A heavy weight settled into my heart. I think I'd known it the night before when I checked on him and hadn't been able to find a pulse. Still, guessing something and knowing it for sure were two different things. It was going to be a long time before I could close my eyes and not see him lying in the snow in front of my car.

I counted the tiles in the floor as we walked simply to keep my mind off of it. I wasn't confident I wouldn't faint again if I mused on it for too long.

As we passed through the foyer, I kept my eyes down and my head ducked. Erik might be in at work today, and this wasn't how I wanted him to see me again after so long—in clothes I'd been wearing for 24 hours, a man's blood on my hands (metaphorically speaking), and still wearing the scarf he'd given me the last time I saw him.

We'd left things in an awkward place when I went back to Virginia. I was only supposed to be gone a week or so, not the two months I'd vanished for. Since

Erik and I had only had two dates before I left, I hadn't been sure of the etiquette and whether calling him regularly would make me seem clingy or stalkerish. We'd exchanged a few emails and some texts, but I wouldn't have called the communication deep or meaningful.

So I did not want him to see me looking like a mess and scare him away before we got a fair chance to rekindle things.

Officer Dornbush ushered me inside the office and even helped me into the chair as if he were afraid my episode from last night would return. Then he went off to find the interim chief.

My hands started to sweat, and I wiped them on my jeans. Hopefully whoever had replaced Carl Wilson as chief would believe me as easily as Officer Dornbush had. My experiences with the Fair Haven police department had been mostly positive in the few weeks I'd spent here prior to my return to Virginia, but I'd be a stranger to the new chief and he'd have no reason to take my word over the officer who locked me up. It wasn't like I could even prove I hadn't been drinking at this point. The officer hadn't administered a breathalyzer or a blood test. A good lawyer could easily get me off if they tried to press charges, but that's not how I'd imagined my return to Fair Haven would go.

The door swooshed open behind me, and I swiveled in my seat to face the interim chief.

It was Erik Higgins.

Chapter 4

Erik looked exactly like he had the last time I saw him. Same linebacker build. Same square jaw. Same military-short haircut. Though the out-of-character stubble on his chin suggested my accident kept him out most of the night.

"You're the new chief?" I blurted.

"Interim chief." His mouth twitched in the this-*is*-my-smile way he had. "Eventually they'll bring in someone more experienced to permanently fill the role."

I held back a flinch. My exclamation had sounded like I didn't think he could handle the job. That wasn't the case. I'd just been surprised to see him. Of course I couldn't say that, either.

I dug around for some of the diplomacy my mom had drilled into me growing up. "It's a testament to your abilities that they put someone so young into the position of interim chief."

The almost-smile faded, and he lowered himself into the chair across the desk from me, his movements slow, like he was dragging dumbbells behind him on a rope. "Thanks. It's a little different than I thought it would be."

I clasped my hands in my lap to keep from squirming. I'd never felt awkward around Erik before, not even when we first met while he was interviewing me about the gas leak in the house I'd inherited from my Uncle Stan. But now the no-man's-land of our relationship left me feeling like a kid called into the principal's office. A defensive kid in a principal's office because I hadn't done anything wrong.

Erik cleared his throat. "Remember how I sometimes have to ask questions because it's part of the job?"

The last time he'd prefaced a string of questions with that caveat, he'd asked if I was suicidal or having money troubles. A teasing retort sprang to my lips, but I swallowed it back down and nodded.

"Keep that in mind." His professional mask was firmly in place now, and with any hint of a smile gone, the dark circles under his eyes grew starker. "Had you had anything alcoholic to drink in the 24 hours prior to the accident?"

"You know I don't drink."

He sighed and propped an arm up on the desk. "Erik knows that Nicole doesn't drink, but I can't deal with this situation as your friend. I have to approach it as a police officer with a potential suspect." His gaze shifted to the other side of the room. "Mostly."

Yeah, most suspects wouldn't have been interviewed in the chief's office. And he hadn't read me my rights. After all the concessions he'd made for me, he didn't need me giving him crap for doing what he needed to do to cover both our butts.

Especially when it was only my hunger pains talking. My stomach said breakfast had passed a while ago. "I'm sorry. What else do you need to ask?"

His shoulders relaxed. "Had you taken any drugs, prescription or otherwise, the day of the accident?"

I shook my head. "Not even an aspirin or a decongestant."

"And did you flee the scene of the accident?" There was a brittleness to his voice, almost like he dreaded my answer.

For the first time, I saw it though his eyes. We'd once talked about how difficult it was to deal with finding guilt in someone you'd hoped was innocent. He probably feared he was facing a situation like that now. "I left the scene, but I wasn't fleeing. I tried to call 9-1-1, but my phone couldn't get a signal, so I covered him with my coat"—I held out my arms to illustrate its absence—"and came straight here. It seemed like the best option for getting him help."

Erik ran a hand over his face. It could have been my imagination, but I thought I heard him mumble *Thank God*. "I need to take an official statement from you. You alright if I record it?"

I gave permission. A recording should mean I didn't have to repeat it all again. The first telling had been hard enough. The second felt like applying pressure to a wound. It might stop the bleeding, but it hurt like heck in the process.

When I reached the part about hitting the man in the street, Erik's jaw clenched slightly. I didn't know him well enough to know what it meant. I focused my gaze on my hands and plowed forward.

I finished with the officer at the front desk locking me in the cell.

A brush of red painted the top of Erik's ears. "He's not an officer. He's a temporary dispatcher, and he's about to be fired."

My stomach dipped. That was great. I could ruin two lives in one blow. "I didn't love spending a night in a cell, but it didn't hurt me."

"Not only did he put your life in danger, but if you had been a drunk driver, he jeopardized any case we would have had against you by violating procedure." He rose to his feet and rolled his shoulders. "We didn't even know he'd put anyone in the cells until Quincey—Officer Dornbush—came in at 9:00."

I saw what he meant now. If I'd killed someone due to my own stupidity rather than due to a freak accident of nature, I'd have walked because of the vigilante actions of one man.

Wait. If Officer Dornbush came in at 9:00...I glanced at my watch. 10:23. No wonder my head felt like someone had hit me with a hammer. I hadn't had anything to eat in over 16 hours. "Am I free to go then?"

Erik nodded.

I shot to my feet and the floor shifted underneath me. I grabbed the edge of the desk. All the stress and no food was clearly not a good combination for me.

Erik was at my side before I even saw him move. He lowered me back into the chair, his hands secure on my arms.

He probably thought I *was* on something now since I couldn't walk straight. "I'm just hungry."

He rested his fingers under my chin and tilted my face up so I had to look him in the eyes. "Follow my finger." He moved it back and forth in front of me, then touched his hand to my forehead. "Your pupils are the same size and you don't feel feverish. I want to have a doctor look you over anyway."

I gently pulled his hand away. As interim chief, he had more important things to do than fuss over me. "Seriously, all I need is a piece of cheese or something."

He gave me a look like granite. If I'd been lying, that look would have made me crack. As it was, I held steady.

He stepped back. "We'll go through a drive-thru on our way to the hospital."

I climbed to my feet more carefully this time. The floor stayed steady. "I don't need a hospital."

He stayed next to me as if prepared to catch me should my legs decide I wasn't as okay as I claimed. "Are you really going to argue with the chief of police?" he asked.

I glanced at him sidelong and tried—unsuccessfully—to hold back a smile. "*Interim* chief."

Half an hour later, I was tucked into the front seat of Erik's police cruiser, wearing his jacket—which could have fit two of me—and eating a chocolate milkshake and large fry. Responsible Nicole would have gotten a salad and a smoothie, but after the last twenty-four hours, responsible Nicole had been too tired to put up a fight when I-want-junk-food Nicole reared her head.

Erik paid for the food and didn't comment on my choices. I'd tried to pay for them myself, but my purse was still MIA. Probably in my impounded car.

We ended up sharing the fries as he drove.

I probably should have allowed myself to enjoy the companionable silence, but I was painfully aware that I was alive and the man I'd hit wasn't. My brain kept skipping back to that fact like it was one of my dad's vintage records. "Who was he?"

It came out softer and more vulnerable than I intended. So soft that I wasn't sure Erik even heard me. He stared straight ahead and a muscle jumped in his jaw.

And then I figured it out. He'd known him.

He'd bought me a scarf and fries and I'd killed someone he knew and cared about.

The air seemed to vanish from the car, and I couldn't catch my breath again. I leaned over and put my head between my knees, but that dizzy, queasy feeling from last night was setting in again.

The car stopped and a large hand rubbed my back in soothing circles. "Deep breaths. Listen to the sound of my voice and take deep breaths."

I breathed in when he told me to and out when he told me to. Slow and steady. My vision started to clear, and I straightened up. He handed me my milkshake, and I sucked in the cold liquid.

"And that," he said, "is why I wouldn't have let you drive yourself yet even if your car wasn't evidence."

I leaned my head back against the headrest. "I'm sorry."

"Don't be too hard on yourself. You've experienced a trauma."

"That wasn't what I meant."

He turned his gaze away from me and looked out the front windshield again. That was for the best. The idea of seeing the same type of disappointment in me on his face that I'd seen on my father's face almost every day of my life was more than I could bear.

The muscle in his jawline bulged again like he was gritting his teeth. "His name was Paul Buchanan. We served together. He's the one who convinced me to move to Fair Haven."

Before I could think of how to respond other than with another apology, Erik's cell phone rang.

He glanced down at it almost like he didn't recognize what it was, then his expression cleared. "I have to take it."

I nodded, my throat suddenly too tight to squeeze out any words at all.

Erik tapped the screen. "Higgins."

A pause. I tried to read his face, but he was too well trained. I picked up nothing. But I thought the voice on the other end of the line might be Mark. Would they have sent an accident victim for an autopsy? I suppose if they'd thought at the time that it was a hit-and-run and that they'd need evidence for court then it made sense.

"I'll be right there." Erik glanced at me. "I have Nicole with me."

Something bled through into his voice that I couldn't interpret. I wanted to pummel the seat cushion. Reading people was what I did. When I encountered someone I couldn't read, it was a bit like being colorblind and then being asked to point out which color swatch was red and which was green. It was even more frustrating when I knew my own emotional investment was causing some of the fog. Those situations proved my parents' condemnation of me as a bleeding heart correct, and I hated proving them right.

I waited quietly while Erik explained to whoever was on the other end—it must be Mark, since the person obviously knew me by name—that I'd been the driver, and that no, I hadn't actually fled the scene.

Erik signed off, slid his phone back into his pocket, and directed the car onto the road again. He pulled a U-turn. "Mark found something on Paul's body that he thought I'd want to see right away."

Chapter 5

What could Mark have found that would merit an urgent phone call? It's not like I'd backed up and hit him a second time to make sure he was dead or anything.

My stomach lurched. Even though I hadn't run over him a second time, someone else might have run over him while I went for help. That could easily make it look like I'd lied and that I'd intentionally hurt the man...Paul. Erik called him Paul. Erik believed me now, but if the evidence showed otherwise, I couldn't blame him for losing confidence in me.

Erik pulled into the parking lot of Cavanaugh Funeral Home and shut the car off. I followed him through the back door of the building.

"What are we doing here?" I whispered, just in case there was a funeral in progress or a bereaved family meeting with Mark's brother, Grant, who owned and ran the family funeral home.

Erik indicated that we should take the hall to the left. "Because our county's small, Mark's office is here. It gives him a convenient place to store and work with the bodies, and saves on transportation costs afterward."

Erik knocked on a door that bore a bronze plaque reading *County Medical Examiner.*

My traitorous heart kicked up a level like I was on a caffeine high. Unlike with Erik, Mark and I had talked or texted almost every day. All the times I'd imagined my reunion with him, none of my fantasies had included Erik watching us. Most of them involved some variation of Mark telling me his wife had left him, and that he was a single man again.

But maybe Erik being here was best. His presence would hold me accountable and keep me from doing anything too stupid and irreversible. I'd had people look at me as an adulteress before. I didn't want that ever again, especially not from Erik. Wherever our relationship went, I wanted him to still respect me, and he was too straight-laced to ever respect a woman who crossed the line with a married man.

The door flew open, and Mark stood in front of me, his dark hair with its bits of gray tousled like he'd been running his hands through it. And suddenly all I wanted was to hide in his arms and pretend like the events of last night hadn't happened. I didn't even care if Erik was watching.

Mark stepped toward me like he planned to grab me up in a hug and let me do just that. My breath snagged on something in my throat, and I choked out a cough.

He stopped in mid-stride, and his trademark dimples disappeared. "Have you seen a doctor?"

I shook my head and started to say I was fine, but I wasn't. It was going to be a long time before I figured out how to deal with the fact that I'd killed someone, even though it'd been unintentional. I'd also never been the first one to see a body. Everybody I'd seen had been prepared by a mortician or was in crime scene photos, and those were hard enough to handle. So the last thing I could say was that I was fine. But I wasn't physically injured at least.

"I'm not hurt," I said.

"We were heading to the hospital," Erik said from behind me, his voice businesslike, almost too much so given the care he'd shown me earlier. "But you said it was urgent."

If I didn't know they were friends, I would have said the eye contact between them was a stare down.

Mark looked away first and turned to me. "Did you want to come along, or would you rather wait here?"

Practically speaking, I should stay behind. As far back as there were records, my family had been doctors and lawyers. I hadn't chosen the legal profession because I had the skill set for it. I'd chosen it because anything remotely medical made me queasy.

But if Mark had found something that would make me look guilty, I wanted to know about it right away and have a chance to discuss it with them before it made it to official legal channels.

"I'll come along."

Mark took us down the hall and stopped outside the door I remembered from when I'd come here to make arrangements for my Uncle Stan's funeral and had insisted upon seeing his body. The door led into the mortuary fridge.

Mark and Erik led the way through the door marked *Staff Only* and stopped beside a body laid out on a gurney. I stuttered to a stop one step inside the room. I'd expected to have more time to prepare myself. When I asked to see Uncle Stan's body, they'd had to bring him out of the fridge. I'd had a moment to steel myself. But Mark must have left Paul's body out in expectation of Erik's arrival.

No way was I going to be a weakling and back out now, though. I drew in a deep breath. The sharp disinfectant aroma of the room bit into my nose and seemed to send courage down through me. I straightened my shoulders and joined the men.

I barely remembered what the man I'd hit looked like. He'd been face-down, and I'd been so concerned with helping him that I hadn't taken much notice of his appearance at the time. Now I got my first clear look.

Even before death, he must have been fair-skinned, and if he'd been standing, I imagine he would have been close to Mark's height, maybe a bit over six feet. He had a gaunt look to him, like a neatly-trimmed version of a scarecrow.

And his name was Paul. I wanted to try to remember it and think of him that way rather than as *the man* or *the body*. It seemed like I owed him that level of respect at least. He might be only a dead body now, but not that long ago he'd been alive and he'd been Erik's friend.

Seeing him there and working through that, something in my brain shifted a bit. I wouldn't call it closure exactly, but it felt like a step in that direction. Like a time would come when thinking about what had happened wouldn't send me over the edge. I just had to hang on until I got there.

"Here's what I called you to see." Mark pulled on a pair of latex gloves, rolled Paul's torso slightly to the side, and pointed with a ball point pen to a tiny spot on the side of Paul's neck. "Do you see that?"

Erik and I both leaned in at the same time and barely avoided cracking our heads together.

My face burned, and I stepped back. I had to remember I was a spectator here and this was his case. "You first, obviously."

He gave me his lip-twitch of a smile, though it was a little tighter than usual. He bent to within a hand's breadth of Paul's neck and squinted. "Is that a needle puncture?"

"And based on the location, it's highly unlikely that it was self-inflicted." Mark lowered Paul back to the table. "The bruising on his body was also post-mortem and consistent with Nicole's car hitting him when he was in a prone position."

Mark mimed a flat body with one hand and my car running into it, like a giant speedbump, with the other.

I stumbled back a step. He was already dead when I hit him? "But he was still warm. He still felt warm."

Mark reached toward me, glanced down at his gloved hands, and retracted his arms partway, like he wasn't sure whether it was more important to comfort me or to keep from touching me with corpse-hands.

"He likely died a few minutes before you came along, so he would have still been warm. I won't know anything more definitive until I get the results back on what was in his blood, but my best guess right now is that he was attacked, stumbled out into the street looking for help, and whatever he'd been injected with killed him."

I rubbed my fingers into my forehead, along the line above my eyebrows, and the tension pooled there started to release. "I didn't kill him."

"You didn't kill him," Mark said.

The lawyerly part of my brain apparently recovered more quickly than the rest of me because all the implications of Mark's declaration were spinning around in my head, demanding attention. "That means someone else did, and my collision with his body meant you've wasted time looking at the wrong crime scene."

Erik already had his phone in his hand. "I'll call the crime scene techs and have them cordon off the animal shelter. It's less than a hundred yards away."

My gaze jumped between the two men. Mark was nodding, but my lack of knowledge about the town meant I wasn't following. "Why the animal shelter?"

Erik was already talking to someone on his phone.

Mark peeled off his gloves and dropped them into a trash can. "Paul was the manager of the local shelter. When the weather forecast called for heavy snow, he'd sometimes sleep in his office to make sure there'd be someone able to take care of the animals in the morning. Given how close his body was to the shelter, it's likely that's what he was doing and that he was attacked there."

I squished my eyes closed. Paul sounded, at least from the little I knew of him, like a decent man. That assessment was strengthened by the fact that he'd been Erik's friend. Why would someone have killed him?

A warm hand slid along the side of my face.

My eyes popped open.

Mark stood in front of me, much too close. He cupped my cheek in his hand. "You didn't do anything wrong, Nikki," he said softly.

My mouth went dry. The man really should have been a movie star instead of a medical examiner, and if he kept looking at me the way he was, I was going to kiss him, right here next to a dead body with Erik standing only a few feet away.

Mark couldn't realize what his touch did to me. He'd admitted to me before that he struggled with social interactions. It was possible he simply didn't know that this wasn't the way you treated a girl who was a friend as opposed to a girlfriend. Although my track record said I might not be the best one to judge a man's sincerity, Mark didn't strike me as the type who would cheat on his wife.

Erik cleared his throat beside us, and I jerked away from Mark's touch. Then I mentally kicked myself. Pulling away like that probably only made us seem more guilty, not less. Not that there was anything to be guilty for. I hadn't actually done anything. I'd only thought about it.

"I'd better take you home." Erik zipped up his jacket. "And I'll have your car towed to Quantum Mechanics."

Tony, the owner of Quantum Mechanics, had done a great job repairing my car when I'd driven it over a fence last fall, so I was confident he could take care of whatever damage I'd done to it last night.

"Thanks." I stifled a yawn. I'd slept a full eight hours or more, but it seemed like the emotional toll of the last day was finally catching up to me. "Home sounds good."

Mark moved in close enough that our arms bumped. "I'll take her home. You probably have a lot of work to do, and I'm in a holding pattern until the test results come in."

Something flashed across Erik's face. I couldn't tell if it was relief, reluctance, or something else entirely— like censure. If I were him, I'd think we were having an affair too. Unintentionally, Mark had made it look like we were a couple, and I'd contributed to it. My reaction to his touch had surely been blazing from my face.

"That's probably for the best," Erik said. "Give me a call when the test results come back."

The fatigue I'd heard before was back in his voice. It was a different situation, but I thought I might know a little how he felt. When Uncle Stan died, my ability to grieve was limited by my need to take care of things and investigate his death. Erik couldn't grieve for his friend now because he had to investigate his murder. The need to hold yourself together made you tired in a way that went far beyond your physical body.

"I'll give you a call if I have any questions," Erik said to me.

Which I couldn't help but notice was different than saying he'd call me, as in call me to talk or call me to ask me out again. He definitely thought Mark and I were having an affair, but there was nothing I could say right now to change his mind—not with Mark standing next to me.

Once he was gone, I talked Mark out of taking me to the hospital, though he did subject me to twenty questions and a quick check over himself to make sure I was okay.

I rotated both arms for him, supposedly the last exercise in his exam. "I wasn't going that fast, you know. It was more the shock of it than anything else."

"Still." He smiled down at me with those heart-melting dimples of his. "I couldn't forgive myself if I let you walk away injured."

Warmth flared in my chest and coursed down through the rest of my body. Mark had this way of looking at me like I was a masterpiece, special and unique and worthy of a pedestal.

That sort of adoration was hard to resist, especially for me. The therapist I'd started seeing after I found out my last boyfriend, Peter, was married and a pathological liar said the slang term for it was *daddy issues*. Since I'd never received the approval I needed from my dad growing up, I lost my better judgment when a man gave it to me now. It's how I'd been so easily tricked by Peter.

And if I wasn't careful, I was going to cross more than emotional lines with Mark because of it.

When Mark was satisfied I wasn't hurt, we headed out for his truck. He helped me up into it and even buckled me in.

I folded my hands in my lap as he walked around to the driver's side. I'd hoped that because we'd kept things light while I'd been gone that this wouldn't be an issue, that we could simply be friends. Turned out, I still couldn't do it. Worse, the way he acted seemed to indicate that my feelings weren't one-sided.

Maybe I had it all wrong. It wouldn't be the first time that I'd mistaken *nice and caring* for *interested.* The one thing I knew for sure was we needed to talk about it. I'd rather look like a fool than risk becoming a willing adulteress. At least with Peter, I hadn't known he was married.

If Mark felt nothing for me beyond friendship, I'd let him decide whether we continued spending time with each other or not. If he felt the way I did, we'd have to break this off.

Mark started the truck and pulled out of the parking lot, heading down the road in the direction of Sugarwood, the maple syrup bush and store I'd inherited from my Uncle Stan.

I quietly drew in a deep breath and sucked my hands up into the sleeves of Erik's coat to hide how much they were shaking. "I think there are some things we need to talk about."

He flashed me his dimples again. "There are, but now's not the time. Right now you need to rest. Do you want to stop and grab something to eat?"

I shook my head. Not only was my appetite completely gone, but I couldn't tell if he knew what I was talking about and wanted to avoid it or if he'd missed my meaning entirely. "I just want to go home and get to sleep."

"Fair enough."

We drove in silence the rest of the way. Mark probably assumed I was too tired to talk. When we pulled up in front of Uncle Stan's—my house, he helped me out of the truck again and walked me to the door.

I pulled my keys from my pocket. Thankfully I hadn't left them in the car or I'd have no way to get into the house.

I went to slide them into the lock, but the door swung open at my touch.

I couldn't think of any good reason why my door would be unlocked. Since I hadn't planned to be gone long, I'd left the electricity and water turned on. There'd been no need for anyone to enter the house to turn them off or back on again.

"Mark," I called, backing up from the door.

He turned back.

When he reached my side, I pointed at the slightly open door. "I think someone's in my house."

Chapter 6

I couldn't catch a freaking break. All I wanted was a hot bath and to climb into bed, and now I had to worry about whether someone had robbed my home, and worse, whether or not they were still in there somewhere.

For a brief moment, I considered banging my head against the wall out of sheer frustration. "Should we call the police?"

"I am the police."

I raised my eyebrows, giving him my best *since when?* look.

Mark shrugged. "I work with the police. Besides, you know how busy they are."

That was true. The last thing Erik needed was me adding yet another thing onto his plate. Besides, it was daylight, and there were two of us. Surely that made it safe enough for us to at least investigate on our own.

I glanced back at Mark's truck. "I don't suppose you carry a gun in that thing."

"Dang it, Jim. I'm a doctor, not a cowboy," he said, in a pretty passable impression of Dr. Leonard McCoy.

I cracked up and slapped both hands over my mouth. Mark turned red in the face like he was holding in laughter as well.

"If there is someone in there, they know we're coming now," I said. "We would never make it as cat burglars."

Mark was still grinning. "I guess it's a good thing we're on the right side of the law, then."

All the mirth drained out of me. Unless we wanted to bother Erik over what might be nothing, we needed to search my house, and I didn't want to go in empty handed. I motioned to Mark to follow me. Uncle Stan had a little shed out back next to his trash cans. I hadn't looked inside when I was here before, but if I knew my uncle, he had rakes and shovels and all those yard-care kinds of things.

I checked inside. Jackpot. I handed Mark the shovel and took the rake for myself.

Mark quirked an eyebrow. "What am I supposed to do? Bludgeon the burglar to death if he's in there?"

I shuddered. Definitely not. I'd seen enough death in the last twenty-four hours.

Mark's face sobered. "I'm sorry. I didn't think."

I waved it away and headed back to the house. Mark stopped me and went in first, shovel held up like a top-heavy baseball bat. I had to hold back a snicker. We looked like we belonged in a slapstick comedy.

I tiptoed in behind him. Mark headed toward the kitchen. I peeled off in the direction of the family room.

The lights were off, but sunlight streamed through the three floor-to-ceiling windows. The room looked empty, but it also held a couch and a recliner that could easily provide a hiding place.

I wiped a damp palm on my jeans. I'd lived alone since graduating from law school, and I'd never once felt afraid in my home. But since Uncle Stan was murdered in this house and I was almost blown up thanks to a man-made gas leak, I found myself a little less confident.

I edged toward the couch. A floor board squeaked beneath my foot. I jumped and a head popped up from the couch.

I screamed and swung, black dots of panic dancing in my vision. My target yelped and ducked.

I recognized the voice. My heart rate dropped back closer to normal, and I lowered my rake. "Russ?"

Russel Dantry's head came back into view, his grey hair mussed up like he'd been napping.

Mark plowed into the room, shovel raised. His gaze hopped to Russ, and he skidded to a stop. "I heard yelling."

Russ scrubbed his hand over his eyes. "Nikki nearly decapitated me."

All the stress of the past day must have been making me giddy. I tried to hold back laughter and snorted instead. "That's what you get for hiding in my house. What are you doing here?"

"Waiting for you." Russ eased to his feet, his movements slow and stiff, a rare sign of his age, and stretched his arms above his barrel-shaped torso. His back cracked. "When you were late and I couldn't get you on your cell, I started to worry. Figured I'd come here and wait so I'd know first thing if you showed up. I must have dozed off somewhere around dawn."

It'd been a long time since anyone had waited up for me to come home. But then again, even in high school I'd been hyper-responsible, setting my own curfew and abiding by it.

Russ' mention of not being able to reach me on my phone reminded me that he wouldn't be the only one worried about me.

"Can I borrow your cell for a second?" I asked Mark. "I should text my mom and my best friend to let them know I made it here safely. They're probably worried, too."

I used Mark's phone to quickly message my mom and Ahanti and let them know that I wasn't sure when

I'd have my phone back. So much of Fair Haven was a cellular dead zone that I might not even miss my phone...at least for a day or two.

Russ came around the couch, and Mark handed him the shovel.

Mark touched his forehead like he was doffing a cap. "Now that we've secured the castle, m'lady, I need to get back to the office. I'll call you later."

He let himself out.

Russ stuck a hand in his pocket and it came out holding a key. "Still have this from when it was your uncle's place." He extended his hand toward me, across the back of the couch. "I can give it back if you want."

Russ had been my Uncle Stan's best friend as well as the manager of Sugarwood. I should have realized he might still have a key to the house, but my mind wasn't super clear right now. Regardless, Russ seemed like my best choice to hold a spare. "Keep it. That way if I get locked out, you can rescue me."

"That's what partners are for."

While I'd been away, I had managed to complete two pieces of important business. I'd taken care of the necessary tasks and paperwork to be able to practice law in Michigan, and Russ and I had signed a partnership agreement, making him half owner of Sugarwood. Since he and Uncle Stan had been talking about doing the same prior to Uncle Stan's death, it'd seemed like the right thing to do.

And, frankly, I needed the help.

Russ nudged me toward the kitchen. "Come on. I'll make you a cup of coffee." He tugged on the sleeve of Erik's coat. "Looks to me like you have a story to tell."

Russ and I had originally planned to start my training in Sugarwood's operations my first day back, but when I nodded off in the middle of a sentence, we postponed for the following day.

"You'll need your energy," Russ had said with a wink.

I didn't have the courage to ask him what he meant.

After Russ left, I'd turned on the hot water for a bath when I realized it wasn't just my cell phone I didn't have. I also had no clean clothes and no toiletries. Uncle Stan probably had some bar soap somewhere, and I could maybe even scrounge up a tube of toothpaste and an unopened toothbrush, but no way was I wearing my dead uncle's deodorant. Or his jammies.

The doorbell rang. I turned off the water and crossed my fingers that it was Russ returning for something he'd forgotten. Maybe he'd drive me to the store for some necessities.

When I opened the door, Officer Dornbush stood outside instead, my largest suitcase and one of the smaller matching ones resting beside him. They were from the purple-and-hot-pink polka dot set I bought specifically because they were easy to identify on the airport luggage carousel, and the long-suffering look on Officer Dornbush's face said that lugging them around had made him as uncomfortable as a man stuck holding his wife's purse.

"The chief thought you might need some of your belongings." Officer Dornbush glanced back over his shoulder as if expecting someone to come up and take his man card away. "Can I bring them inside? Please."

"Did you wear wool socks like I told you to?" Russ asked the next morning when I met him at the small rental shop next to Short Stack, Sugarwood's pancake house. It was a good thing I didn't have a lisp or the names would have given me a complex. As it was, I'd have to avoid trying to say them too fast if I didn't want to accidentally spit on the person I was talking to.

I nodded in response to Russ' question, and he handed me a pair of waterproof boots and what looked like nylon land fins.

"I guessed at your size," he said.

I took off my running shoes and laced on the boots. They fit perfectly. I had no idea what to do with the fins.

One of the first things Uncle Stan had done when he purchased the property years ago was to find ways to make it more profitable. Along with establishing Short Stack, he'd also cleared and maintained nine miles of trails. The trails were free to use, but Sugarwood did a bustling business renting cross-country skis and snowshoes to tourists in the winter months.

The things Russ handed me didn't look like any of the snowshoes I'd seen in pictures. Those were made of wood and lattice.

"Uh, Russ." I held up a fin in each hand. "What exactly are we doing today? Because if these are for polar bear dipping, I'm out of here."

"We're checking the lines that carry the sap from the trees to the storage tanks during sugar season. They can be damaged by falling branches and other things during the offseason, so we have to repair them every year before the sap starts to flow." He took the fins from me and tucked them under his arm. "These are to keep you from having to wade through knee-high snow to do it."

So they were snowshoes. Modern snowshoes. Better than fins this time of year, but I still foresaw a day spent outside. I'd have to call Erik later and thank him for the delivery of my bags. My warm clothes and hat had been inside, and I'd clearly need them today. My coat was still MIA, so I'd grabbed one of Uncle Stan's from the hall closet.

"Nikki?" Russ called from the door. "You coming?"

I hurried after him. He added my snowshoes and a set of poles that looked like they could have also been used for cross-country skiing to a sled that he'd hooked up to the back of a snowmobile.

I'd never ridden on a snowmobile before. A little bubble of excitement built in my stomach. "We're taking that?"

Russ nodded. "We're working part of the grid on the far side of the bush today." He swung a leg over the snowmobile and hooked a thumb over his shoulder. "Hop on."

The snowmobile skimmed over the snow like a boat over waves. The wind bit at my cheeks, but this time the sting was worth it. My teeth started to ache from the cold, and I realized it was because I was grinning. So this was why people chose to live where there was a lot of snow. This I could get used to.

Russ finally eased the snowmobile to a stop. He helped me snap into my snowshoes and then belted a utility belt around my waist that contained a small bottle of water, a pouch with a map and marker for tracking any damaged pipe, and a black box with a short antenna.

I pulled the box out. "What's this?"

Russ gave me an are-you-kidding-me look. "It's a walkie-talkie."

My blank expression must have given me away.

He pushed the button on the side of his matching box. "It's a two-way radio."

His words came out of the handset in my hand. "So basically it's like an antique cell phone," I said.

Russ slowly shook his head. "Kids today." But a smile peeked out. "A little bit. It doesn't depend on radio towers, so we're safe from the dead zones, and you have to be on the same frequency as the person you want to talk to."

He gave me more instructions on using the walkie-talkie and the poles that went along with my snowshoes and then explained what to look for in the sap lines.

He turned back toward the snowmobile. "Keep heading south," he motioned ahead of him with his arm, "and we should meet back up in about an hour."

The whir of the snowmobile faded as he drove away, and the only sounds breaking the silence were the top branches of the maples tapping together in the breeze and the schew-weh-weh-weh-weh call of the cardinal perched high in a bare maple tree a few feet from me.

I drew in a deep breath. The air was sharp and bright. Even after a rain or a fresh snow, the air in DC never smelled this clean. Despite my inauspicious return to Fair Haven, moments like this reminded me why I'd come.

I tromped forward, trying to use my poles the way Russ had shown me to keep my balance. I was barely an eighth of the way into the route marked on my map before sweat dampened the collar of my jacket. I was an avid biker and enjoyed the martial arts-based workout classes at my gym back in Virginia, but this used an entirely different set of muscles. How did Russ maintain his barrel shape if this was how he spent his days?

I propped my poles against a tree and checked the next length of line. So far, I hadn't encountered anything that I'd need to mark for Noah, our repair man.

I stepped forward to follow the line around a bend, one snowshoe caught on the other, and I toppled over sideways. Snow swooshed up into my face, sending an instinctive scream from me.

Eyes squished shut, I swiped it away. At least no one was around to see my clumsiness this time.

I blinked my eyes open again. I'd face planted a few feet from a ring of packed down snow. Red splatters, like paint thrown from a brush, stained the greyish white ground.

My breath caught in my throat. It looked like a crime scene.

Chapter 7

"Russ?"

I let go of the button on the walkie-talkie and listened. No reply.

"Russ?"

Still nothing.

"Russ? Please answer." A note of panic entered my voice.

"You forgot to say *over*, Nikki." Russ' voice sounded like he was speaking from an empty room, tinny but clear. "I didn't know you were done. Over."

I blew out a breath of air. That was great. I was sounding hysterical again. *Be a grownup, Nicole.*

"I think someone might have been murdered out here. There's a packed down section of snow and blood." I let go of the button. Then pressed it again. "Over."

"It was probably just an animal."

Russ' voice was patient, and for a second, I almost forgot I was talking to him rather than my Uncle Stan. Uncle Stan had always been the voice of reason to my wild ideas.

"We have wolves and coyotes here in the winter," Russ said. "It's sad when you run into a spot where they've killed something, but it's nature. Over."

The ring of packed down snow seemed too wide for that, but it made more sense than my theory. After all, a murderer wouldn't be rolling around on the ground with their victim out here in the woods and packing down the snow.

I shook my head. I couldn't keep doing this. First I thought someone had broken into my house. And now I was fabricating murders in the woods. All because I knew there'd been another murder in Fair Haven and the murderer was still walking free.

No way could I go on like this for weeks or months without any idea of where the investigation was even at. Somehow I had to convince Erik to let me join in. At least then I'd feel like I was actively doing something rather than sitting by and hoping the murderer wouldn't strike again.

I paced the length of my kitchen and back again, staring down my cell phone as it lay on the counter. Thanks to Erik, my purse had also come back with Officer Dornbush last night.

So I *could* call Erik—it was a physical possibility—but first I needed to gather my nerve and plan out what to say. I didn't want it to seem like I was only interested in talking to him now that I was back and needed something.

Plus, he didn't owe me anything. I couldn't come up with one good reason why he should allow me to be a part of this investigation.

I grabbed the phone and flopped down onto the couch. Maybe that was the answer. Erik was a straightforward kind of guy. I'd just ask him and explain why. No manipulation. No lies. No omissions.

The worst he could do was say no.

Well, not entirely. I ruffled my hand through my snowmobile-helmet hair. The worst he could do was think I was fabricating reasons to spend time with him, and then I'd come across as needy. I did *not* want to earn a reputation for being the kind of woman who trumped up reasons to spend time with someone in the vain hope that, if I hung around enough, the guy would see how amazing I was and want to date me. That'd probably backfire in my face even if I had wanted to try. The more time he spent with me, the more chances I'd have to trip over my own feet or say something uber-nerdy.

Stop being a baby and just call him already.

I dialed the cell number I still had stored in my phone. One ring. Two. Three. If it went to voice mail, should I leave a message or hang up?

"Higgins."

I fumbled the phone, grabbed it in midair, and swept it back to my ear. "Umm, hi. It's me." Which could be anyone if he didn't recognize my voice. It'd be humiliating for me if he had to ask. "Nicole." What if he knew more than one Nicole? "Nicole Fitzhenry-Dawes."

He chuckled into the phone with that gravelly soft way he had. "I knew which *me* it was," he said. "Did Quincey bring your bags?"

I told him that he had and thanked him for thinking of it. "Did you get the test results back on what might have been in the syringe?"

He might think it was strange that I was calling him rather than Mark to find out, since it'd been clear from Mark's reception yesterday that we'd kept in touch, but it was the best way I could think of to lead softly into what I wanted to ask.

"The results came back about an hour ago. Mark's a miracle worker for getting the lab in Grand Rapids to rush results on tests he can't run himself. Paul was injected with pentobarbital."

It was the drug used by some states in lethal injection executions. A high dose caused a person's lungs to stop working. "That's highly regulated, isn't it? Are you able to trace people in this area who've purchased it?"

Erik's sigh carried through the phone. "Yeah, but I suspect that won't lead us anywhere. Pentobarbital is also used by animal shelters. Fair Haven's shelter is no-kill, but they still keep a supply on hand for animals who are too sick or too aggressive to adopt out. And the cabinet where it's stored was unlocked. Paul could have been killed with pentobarbital from the shelter. We have no way of knowing since we didn't find the syringe itself."

That potentially narrowed their field of suspects in a different way. "Do you think he was killed by some-one who worked at the shelter?"

"I have officers out interviewing all the staff and volunteers, but you know how it is. No one's going to come right out and admit to having a motive for killing Paul."

You know how it is. His words wrapped like a warm blanket around me. Those were words for someone he at least viewed as a knowledgeable equal. I might not be a law enforcement officer, but he knew I'd been a criminal lawyer and had at least some experience with how things worked.

And he'd given me the perfect way in to the investi-gation. This wasn't the kind of case where an actual officer from another town would be spared to go "un-dercover," working with the people at the shelter. But that's exactly what Erik needed—someone they wouldn't associate with the police, so they wouldn't feel a need to hide how they really felt about Paul, their anger issues, or any other dirty laundry that could have caused this. I was the only person in town with no known history. I could become whatever I needed to be to get them talking. It was what I was good at, after all.

The happiness still curling around my heart from Erik's earlier words hardened and an ache built in my chest. If I offered now, he'd think I was doing it for him. And I would be. I did want to do something to help him. But I'd also be doing it for me. How much would my mixed motives matter to him?

"You still there?" he asked.

"They might admit it to someone they don't know." I spit the words out before I could second guess myself any more. "And they're short-staffed now, right? And I've always loved animals."

It came out a little more garbled than I'd intended.

He paused for so long that I was sure he saw right through me. "You don't have to worry about this, Nicole. You have enough to do running Sugarwood."

I ran a nail along the seams in the couch. Was that meant as a nice mind-your-own-business? Or was he truly concerned about me stretching myself thin?

The only way to know was to tell him the truth. "I want to help. For Paul. For my own piece of mind."

"Promise me you won't go investigating on your own?" I swear I could hear a smile in his voice. How could that man smile with his voice and not with his lips?

I bounced a little on the couch. "Cross my heart and hope to..." Drat. Very bad choice of words.

"Hope to live a long and happy life?" Erik filled in.

"Exactly." I shifted my phone to the other ear and tapped a finger on the back. Please say yes. Please, please, please. "I had enough excitement last fall. I'll only be there as your eyes and ears. If I sense anything is off, I'll bring it to you."

There was another long pause on his end. "Alright."

"Thank you."

I chewed my bottom lip. I should take this moment and tell him that Mark and I weren't having an affair. If I did that, though, it was also akin to hinting I wanted him to ask me out again.

"I'll pick you up at eight tomorrow morning," he said before I could dig my courage out from between the couch cushions. "That'll give me time to let you in, show you around, and be gone before Craig, the assistant manager, gets in at 9:00. You can wait outside. Tell him Paul hired you."

A voice said something in the background.

"Gotta go," Erik said. "See you tomorrow."

He disconnected before I could even say goodbye.

I slumped back into the couch cushions and smiled. I was officially on the case.

Chapter 8

Snowshoeing was from the devil. When I woke up the next morning, my body ached all over like I had the flu. My muscles loosened a little after a hot shower, but when Erik's unmarked police car pulled up outside my house, I was still moving like an old woman.

He jogged over to me. "You *are* hurt from the crash."

I picked my way down the steps. "I don't even have a seatbelt bruise from the crash. This is what happens when you're too stubborn to admit that a sixty-year-old man can outwork you."

Erik chuckled and adjusted his pace down the paving stone walkway to match mine. "I ran into Russ this morning at The Burnt Toast. He was moving like he fell off a ladder. He said he didn't want to stop yesterday before you did because he didn't want you to think he was too old for the job. Sure you two aren't related?"

Once we were in the car, he headed out of Sugarwood's long driveway and into town. He turned off before we reached the road for the shelter.

I twisted slightly in my seat. We were headed in the same direction as we had been before Mark called us the day after the accident. "You're not still trying to take me to the hospital, are you?"

"Quantum Mechanics. I thought we could get you another load of your belongings, and you could talk to Tony about how long you're going to be without your car this time."

I tried not to cringe at the *this time*—and failed. The gossip mill in this town spread news faster than a cold spread in a pre-school. Truth be told, I would have been more surprised if Erik hadn't heard about the fence I'd managed to jam up into the underside of my car previously. Still, that didn't make it any less humiliating.

The inside of Quantum Mechanics smelled like burnt coffee, rubber, and gasoline. A chemical headache burst to life in my temples. If running Sugarwood failed for me, I knew one place I definitely wasn't coming for a job.

Erik tapped the tiny *Ring for Service* bell perched on the counter, and Tony appeared from the back, wiping his palms on a grey cloth and a black smear covering his bald head as if he'd scratched his scalp with a hand he didn't realize was covered in grease.

Tony did his awkward shuffle with no eye contact as he prepared the paperwork for me to sign.

As he slid it across the counter, he peeked at me. "I could add rubber bumper car bumpers onto your car if you're going to make this a regular thing. It'd cost a lot less for you in the long run."

Erik snickered and I tossed him a just-keep-laughing-mister look.

He backed slowly away. "I think I'll go get some of those boxes from your car now."

I signed the paperwork and didn't even ask about a rental since I'd learned last time that no one in Fair Haven ever expected one.

We were back on our way to the animal shelter within ten minutes. Erik unlocked the door with the key the police still had from their search.

The entrance of the shelter was small—two chairs and a reception desk. It was too cool inside for me to feel comfortable without a coat, but that seemed to be the norm here. My internal thermostat was set to Virginia temperatures rather than the colder climate of Michigan. I might have to accept that I'd never feel warm again.

The air smelled faintly of cat litter, damp dog, and disinfectant—three smells I'd take any day over the odor of the garage.

Erik led the way down one of the two halls that branched off from the entrance.

"This was Paul's office." He opened a door into a room not much bigger than a walk-in closet. Filing cabinets lined the walls. "We've already gone through the contents, but without context, everything seemed normal."

I nodded and continued after him as he pointed out an even tinier break room with a microwave and mini-fridge and a couple of rooms where prospective pet owners could spend some one-on-one time with the animal they were thinking of bringing home.

The horseshoe-shaped hallway eventually took us into the kennel area. Erik had been talking nearly constantly since we'd walked in, explaining things he thought might be worth paying attention to during the time I worked here, like the supplies of antibiotics and other drugs that could be skimmed.

Now he stopped, and his throat worked like he wanted to keep talking but couldn't.

It must have been here. This must have been the spot.

"There were signs of a struggle"—he pointed to the left where there was a hamper of dirty blankets, a washer and dryer, and a silver exam table—"and we found the logbook for the pentobarbital. Their supply is one syringe short. Best guess is this is where it happened."

His voice cracked.

Panic clawed up my own throat. For my parents, emotions were things you had in private where no one could see you. I barely knew how to handle my own, let alone someone else's, especially someone I'd started to think of as an unshakeable rock.

He scrubbed a knuckle across his upper lip. "Paul was a good man. When this gets out, people are going to start to talk and wonder what he was into that got him killed. I think that's what bothers me the most."

My lack of experience left me with no idea about the best words to say. In lieu of speaking, I rested a hand on his arm and squeezed.

He twitched a little, then his gaze dropped down to my hand with an expression like he thought it might bite him. Maybe he'd been talking more to himself than to me and he'd forgotten I was there. That made sense, right? Whatever the reason, that look found the spot inside me that liked to tell me how unworthy I was and poked it. Hard.

I dropped my hand and stepped back.

An electronic bell dinged up front.

The expression on Erik's face flattened back into the cop mask. "Craig's early. I'll have to sneak out the back."

Then he was gone, leaving me still mired in a whirlpool of emotions I had no idea how to start swimming out of.

Craig turned out to be the veterinary technician who worked on staff at the animal hospital, as well as the assistant manager. I would have described him as so average he'd blend into a crowd if it hadn't been for the large gap between his front teeth. It was so large that I'd thought he was missing a tooth at first.

I wasn't sure he completely believed my story that Paul had just hired me and had also given me a key to the shelter so I could wait inside for Craig to arrive and train me. But since he couldn't prove otherwise, he gave me the tour again. This time, instead of being focused on what might have led to Paul's death, I learned about how the shelter ran and what my responsibilities would be.

We started to work on feeding the animals and cleaning the kennels. I tried to give each animal a little attention as well as physical care. A black-and-white kitten in one of the cages tried to climb into my arms as soon as I opened the door. I rubbed her chin and her tiny purr vibrated her entire body. By the end of the first day, I was probably going to want to take at least half of them home with me.

I carried the kitten's dishes over to the sink and food containers. "So will Paul be in later today?"

I tried to keep my voice casual. I didn't want him to suspect I already knew Paul was dead. A little voice in my head whispered that if he'd had nothing to do with Paul's death I was being cruel—making him tell me about Paul's passing—but Erik allowed me to come here for a reason.

Then again, why would I be asking if Paul would be in? I'd already told him Paul gave me the key so I could wait for Craig inside. "He said something about still needing to put me into the payroll system."

That sounded plausible and should also explain why he wouldn't be able to find any record of me yet.

Craig had a scoop of dog food halfway to the dish he was holding. "I guess most people wouldn't have heard yet. Paul passed away this week."

I didn't have to fake the sadness on my face. I let what was naturally inside flow out. "What happened?"

"I don't know how much I'm allowed to say, but the police think someone killed him."

I turned my mouth into an O and catalogued that fact that he'd hinted at knowing more than he was possibly able to say. It was a classic phrase for people who wanted to make themselves sound important.

I replaced the kitten's dishes. The kitten finished off the row I'd been working on. Craig was already halfway through the next row, so I moved over to the large dog kennels along the wall. "That's awful that someone would do that."

I unlatched the first door. The dog inside looked to be nearly 80 pounds of muscle, but he stood low to the ground, with short, powerful legs. Beautiful tan and white markings highlighted his face. As I opened the door, a line of hair stood up on the back of his neck. I hated to think what kind of past treatment would have built that reaction to humans into him.

I reached for his dishes. Behind me, I could hear Craig's footsteps headed my way. I wouldn't push for too much info right now. That'd probably make him suspicion. I did want to try to get an initial read, though. "Why would someone want to hurt Paul? He seemed like such a nice man."

A vice-like grip clamped around my arm.

Chapter 9

Craig yanked me backward.

I lost my footing and tumbled to the floor. My heart raced up into my throat. Holy crap. Was this guy a psycho? I'd barely mentioned Paul.

He slammed the kennel door shut as the dog rammed into it, teeth bared.

Heat flared in my cheeks. Apparently I'd gotten more cynical and suspicious than I realized. He hadn't been attacking me because I asked him about Paul. He'd been saving me from being bitten.

A small line of sweat trickled down the side of his face, and he cursed. "Didn't you look at the tag?" He whacked a plastic-coated rectangle hanging from the kennel door and it bounced. "The red dot means *biter,* remember. You need to open the metal door at the back and wait for them to go outside before you enter the kennel."

I'd been so distracted trying to dig for information about Paul that I hadn't even noticed the tag. And he *had* told me. Red was for an animal that was aggressive.

"I'm sorry." I crawled to my feet, keeping well back from the cage where the dog still snarled at us. "I'll be more careful next time."

The electronic bell sounded from the front.

Craig sighed. "Why don't you go take care of that, and I'll finish back here."

I didn't blame him for not trusting me in the back alone. If he hadn't been there...I shuddered. Best not to think about what might have happened if he hadn't been there.

When I reached the entrance area, a stocky woman in a long dress covered in orange flowers riffled through a drawer of the front desk. The dress hung on her in a shapeless mass that had to add at least ten pounds to her frame.

I hesitated at the end of the hall. It's possible she was another employee or a volunteer, but the schedule I'd seen taped to the wall showed only Craig and Paul on for today. Still, it was possible Craig had called in someone else, knowing Paul was dead.

"Excuse me." I stepped up beside her. "May I help you?"

She straightened calmly, slid the door closed, and thrust out her hand. "Bonnie Blythe. I'm so glad to see a fresh face around here."

Her actions said *I belong*, and her words were ambiguous. I still couldn't tell if she were an employee or not. "Do you work here as well?"

She fluttered her hands up into the air. "Geez-o-pete, no. Though I'd be good at it if I did. I have a big heart for animals."

Okaaay. So that made it sound like she was here to adopt. I pulled open the drawer she'd been fishing through. "Were you looking for an adoption form? I can get you all set up."

She made a negative *mm-mm* sound. "I don't need to adopt. I'm here because I heard the manager'd finally gone, and I thought maybe whoever took his place would be more helpful."

She pulled a picture from her backpack-sized purse and slid it to me along the desk. The image showed Bonnie sitting on a white porch with a fawn-colored Bullmastiff hunkered down next to her feet. The dog wore a blue bowtie around its neck.

She tapped the photo with her finger. "That's my Toby. He went missing, and I've been coming here every day trying to get someone to help me find him. But that former manager kept telling me they don't look for missing pets. It don't seem right to me. If the animal shelter won't help us find our lost pets, where are we supposed to go?"

I could only imagine how heartbreaking it must be to lose a pet and not know what to do to find him. The police certainly couldn't take on the task. "It does seem like it should be something that the shelter helps with."

"Exactly." She threw her hands up in the air. "I knew when I saw you that you'd be one who'd understand. Not like that Paul. Do you know he actually threatened to ban me if I kept 'pestering'"—she made air quotes around the word—"him?"

I picked up the picture of Toby to buy myself a little time. Maybe I'd been coming at this wrong. If you wanted to find out the truth about a person, sometimes you needed to talk to someone who disliked them. Their friends would often try to protect their memory. Hadn't Erik said as much? He couldn't stand the idea that people would be assuming the worst about Paul.

But we all had secrets, and an enemy would be all too happy to speak ill of the dead.

Not that this woman was necessarily an enemy, but there didn't seem to be any love between them either.

"Nicole? What's taking so long up here?"

I turned around. Craig stood at the end of the hallway, an annoyed expression on his face. I wasn't winning any brownie points with him today. First I'd nearly gotten myself attacked by a dog because I wasn't paying attention, and now he likely thought I was wasting time chatting while he did all the hard work.

I held the picture of Toby out toward him. "Ms. Blythe came in to see if we might have heard anything about her dog. I was helping her."

Then I noticed his annoyed expression was directed more at Bonnie than at me. "Paul told you we'd call if we found out anything about Toby."

Bonnie took a step forward, her hands outstretched. "Yes, but—"

"Now's really not a good time, Bonnie."

Her face twisted in a mixture of anger and hurt, like someone deciding whether to break into tears or throw a punch.

I gritted my teeth so hard pain spiraled up my jaw line. I could see how Bonnie's chatty nature and...persistence could grate on people, but she was still a person with feelings, and he was doing to her exactly what had upset her so much in the past.

A slew of scathing rebukes for Craig ran through my mind, but I drew in a calming breath. Craig was probably grieving and under a lot of stress right now, trying to fill Paul's role. Plus, there'd been a hint of an ego in our conversation earlier, which meant that if I stood up to him, he might well "fire" me. I couldn't afford to lose this job before I'd found out anything useful to Erik.

Craig had crossed his arms over his chest, and Bonnie was sliding her photo of Toby back into her purse, her shoulders hunched but her eyes shooting laser darts at Craig.

There had to be some solution here. Was there a spot where what they both wanted intersected? "I was actually thinking I could help set up a better system to locate lost pets that wouldn't take up the shelter's time."

"Not on paid time," Craig said.

Despite his rescue of me, the man was making it really hard to like him. "No, on my own time."

Bonnie spun me around and crushed me into a hug that smelled like talcum powder and lilies. She held me so tight that if I'd been a few inches shorter, she might have smothered me in her bosom. Behind me, Craig mumbled something about hurry up because we had a lot of work to do and that he'd be waiting for me in the back.

He might not have actually mumbled. My ears might have just been blocked by Bonnie.

When she finally let me go, I stumbled back a step.

"I can't thank you enough," she gushed.

I moved back in case she decided to grab me up again. "Are there many others who are in the same position who might be willing to join us?"

She hugged her purse as if she still needed to clutch something to her. "A bunch of dogs went missing this year right before tourist season."

"So had the former manager put anything in place to help that we could build on?"

She fluttered her hands again, reminding me a bit of a bird trying to take flight. "He kept a file of pets reported missing so he could check when any new animals come in, but that was it."

That wasn't much. It still meant no one was looking for the lost pets. I didn't have any good solutions yet, but I did like a good problem to solve. "Why don't we set up a meeting where we could all brainstorm ideas?"

And where I could casually ask more questions about Paul.

Bonnie dug around in her purse, bringing it up to her face like she might stick her whole head inside. "Just let me find an ink pen to write down your phone number."

The rest of the morning was, thankfully, uneventful, but Craig also avoided me, assigning me to unpacking creates of donated blankets and canned cat food and then checking the expiration dates on all the food on the shelves. It wasn't exactly what I'd envisioned when I'd offered to work here, and it gave me no opportunity to make any progress on Paul's murder.

Sometime around noon, Craig knocked on the edge of the wooden shelf next to where I was shoving new cans of food as far back as possible. I jumped and banged my head off the shelf above. I stumbled backward and rubbed the insta-bump on my skull.

Craig actually cracked a smile at me. "I'm getting the idea that you're just clumsy overall."

If that was his olive branch, I'd take it, even if it was a bit of a backhanded compliment. I needed him to warm up to me. "You could say that. I trip over imaginary things sometimes. The bruises are still real."

His smile warmed up a touch more. "It's time to walk some of the dogs. Want to join?"

The cold air would probably help the ringing in my ears. I grabbed the old coat of Uncle Stan's that I'd brought with me from the closet. The coat was plaid and much too big for me, but it was better than trying to brave the cold in one of my spring jackets. I should ask Erik about getting my coat back, but the idea of wearing a coat I'd left lying over a dead man made me queasy.

"Pick one with a green dot," Craig said while he slid on his own coat. "The more we can work with the adoptable ones, the better their chances of finding a home."

I walked along the rows, giving a wide berth to the kennel of the dog who'd wanted to eat me that morning. Growing up, since my parents wouldn't let me have a pet, I'd read everything I could find on animals, cats and dogs in particular. At the time I was living vicariously through fantasy, but now bits of what I'd studied were coming back to me and making it fun to try to guess what breeds might be mixed up in each of the dogs.

I stopped at the end. A black-and-white ball lay curled up in the corner. I knelt down and the puppy inside lifted her head. A Great Dane by the looks of her. Danes had been my favorite dogs since I'd seen my first Scooby-Doo cartoon.

I reached for the latch and stopped. I'd almost forgotten to check the dot color again. I flipped the tag holder on the door, but it was blank. No information at all and no dot.

"Craig?"

He came around the corner, two tattered leashes dangling from his hand.

I pointed at the kennel. "This one's not color-coded yet."

He sighed. "I meant to have you enter her into the system this morning, then forgot with the Bonnie intrusion. She must have come in late the day Paul died and he didn't have a chance to..." He threw a leash at me. "Pick a different one and we'll deal with her later."

I missed the leash and had to scoop it up off the floor. I bit my cheek to keep from back-talking. If I were a cat, I'd be on my last life with Craig, and he struck me as the kind of man whose ego needed stroking if I wanted to get along with him. He'd perked right up when I'd been self-deprecating.

I opened the kennel of a dog whose wavy, reddish fur made her look like she had some Irish setter in her. She pranced along beside me, and we followed Craig and a terrier-like dog out the back door.

"Thank you for being so patient with me today." I offered the Setter enough slack to sniff around, but not enough to get her into trouble with the Terrier. "The shelter is lucky to have you to replace Paul. I bet they'll make you manager. I'm actually surprised you weren't already."

He leveled a flat gaze at me. "You're not my type."

I stuttered to a stop. The Setter tugged hard on the leash, nearly tipping me over. "Excuse me?"

"You're not my type. I like my women with more brains."

Jerk. The last thread of my patience unraveled. I was done for the day. If I had to stay around this man for any longer, I was going to say something I *wouldn't* regret. And it was fast becoming obvious that I wasn't going to get any information out of him. Unless I was able to work with someone else, this might all be a waste of time.

At least I could still go through Paul's office, and with Craig busy walking dogs, I wouldn't have to explain to him what I was doing. I just needed an excuse to go back inside.

I shivered. It was only half pretend. "It's a bit cold out here for me. Would it be alright if I went inside and added that puppy to the system?"

Craig waved a hand in my direction. "Fine. If you can't figure the system out, there's an instruction manual in the top left drawer."

I put the Setter away and opened the Dane puppy's kennel. She cowered back in the corner. It could be a sign that she'd been abused, but it might also be a result of the strange surroundings. Since I only knew what I'd read in books and online, the nuances of what each breed of dog was like in person were foreign to me.

I sat next to the wall across from her. I'd let her come to me.

She crept slowly from the cage. Seeing her standing up, she was already bigger than I thought—a good forty-five pounds at least. Her white body with black spots made her look at bit like a stocky Dalmatian except for the oversized paws. The spot over her left eye circled around like a bandit's mask.

Once her nose touched my hand, I stroked her head and down her back. It was like the gentle touch snapped her resistance. She crawled into my lap and snuggled her head against my arm. She let out a little sigh.

I let her stay there for a minute, but Craig would be back in to swap dogs any time now. I attached the leash to her collar and walked her back to Paul's office.

Purebred dogs were usually microchipped, so finding her owner, if she had one, shouldn't be that difficult. That should leave me enough time to poke around.

I figured out how to use the chip scanner and a number popped up. Paul had all the information for how to access the online database on a paper in the operating procedures manual, so I had a name and phone number within five minutes.

The shelter only had a phone at the front desk and in the back, so I used my cell phone instead of leaving the office. When I called, I got voicemail and left a message. It wasn't until I'd disconnected that I realized I'd accidentally left my cell phone number as a call back rather than the shelter number. Assuming Craig didn't fire me at the end of the day, that shouldn't matter.

I printed off a kennel tag and added a yellow dot. Then I couldn't help myself. I sat on the floor and played with her for a few minutes more before getting down to the real work—searching through Paul's files for anything important.

I started with the bottom drawer and worked my way up. This cabinet seemed to be invoices for things like food and cat litter, and the accompanying records from the account the shelter used for business purposes.

Everything matched, from the amounts ordered, to amounts delivered, to how much was paid from the account. If Paul had been doing something shady that got him killed, it didn't look like it was via the shelter's financials. I was no forensic accountant, but given the consistency of all the withdrawals for the past six months, it didn't look like Paul was skimming money either.

I returned the paperwork to the drawer. The Dane puppy had fallen asleep curled into a ball by the desk. I gave her another quick ear rub on the way by. Her owners must be crazy with worry. Hopefully they got my voicemail soon and could come for her.

The top drawer of the next filing cabinet was full of folders about missing pets. I pulled out all the files and set them on the desk to take home with me for my "pet" project with Bonnie. It was probably a good thing no one had been around when I'd thought up that corny joke or I might have been tempted to tell it and laugh a little too hard.

The door swung open and both the puppy and I jumped.

Craig stood in the doorway, his coat still on and a leash in his hand. If he was done, I must have been in here longer than I thought. I glanced at the clock and had to hold back a flinch. It was nearly three o'clock.

Craig planted his hands on his hips. "What have you been doing?"

I couldn't tell him what I'd really been up to. Since the best lies were at least partly true, I'd go with that. I pointed at the operations manual. "Studying up. I've figured out how to enter animals into the system and also how to order supplies."

Some of the *got ya* drained from his stance. The disappointed look on his face made me suspect he was looking for an excuse to get rid of me, and he'd probably thought he'd caught me wasting time.

I snagged the puppy's new tag off the desk. "I'll take her outside and then put her away. Did you need me to work on something else?"

Craig shook his head. "Clock out early today. I'll handle the evening feeding. I've got a couple euthanasias today on dogs who are too aggressive to adopt out, and I'm guessing you don't want to be here for that."

I shuddered. Definitely not. "I'll call for my ride as soon as I get this girl settled."

I took care of the puppy quickly, called Russ, and grabbed my coat and purse.

I had the front door open when I remembered that the lost pets' files I needed were still sitting on Paul's desk. I let the door fall closed and turned back.

The hallway down to Paul's office was angled in such a way that I could catch glimpses of Craig in the kennel. My cringe reflex wanted me to close my eyes, but it wasn't like I'd see anything. All he was doing at the moment was grabbing a muzzle from where they hung on the wall and moving toward the dog who'd nearly attacked me earlier today.

I wouldn't have to worry about forgetting his dot color tomorrow, though that hadn't really been an issue. An ache grew in my chest, and I ducked into Paul's office. I needed to get out of here fast. It hurt too much to know what was about to happen.

I grabbed up the files. A heavy thunk-clank carried from the kennel to the office.

That was odd. The only thing back there that could make that distinctive dull thunk-clank was the back door. It didn't have a bell like the front door, probably because workers were always going in and out, walking the dogs.

What the heck was Craig doing? Surely he didn't euthanize dogs outside. Wouldn't he do it right in their kennels to minimize the risk?

I set the file folders back down, hurried through the kennel area, and eased the back door open a crack.

Craig stood at the edge of the empty back lot, where it butted up to the back parking lot. The dog who'd tried to attack me stood muzzled, held at a distance from him by a long dog-catcher's pole with a loop on the end.

He flicked his wrist like he was checking his watch and tapped his foot a couple of times. Who would he be waiting for with one of the dogs he'd supposedly been planning to euthanize?

A navy blue van with splatters of mud and rust along the bottom edges rolled to a stop in front of him. The man who climbed out had long hair pulled back in a ponytail, an angular nose, and a beanie on his head. He looked more like an artist than a meet-in-a-dark-alley type.

I leaned in to see if I could read the license plate. Telling Erik that I saw an old blue van wasn't going to narrow his suspect pool down much if this was related.

My coat snagged on a rough piece of metal at the edge of the door. I wiggled the fabric, but it held fast. I bit back a curse. I was stuck.

I peeked out the crack again. I couldn't see the dog anymore. Craig would be back here any second, and considering how much he already disliked me, it was a pretty sure bet that he wasn't going to believe any excuse I could come up with in the next five seconds for how I got caught on the back door frame.

My heart fluttered with the erratic moth-caught-in-a-glass-jar feeling. I gave a hard tug, and the fabric ripped. I crab-scrambled backward, but it was too late.

The door opened, and Craig loomed over me.

Chapter 10

Craig yanked the door shut behind him and cursed. "What are you still doing here?"

He must have thought I was gone because I'd opened the front door. He would have heard the chime. Since I hadn't actually gone out, though, there hadn't been an accompanying chime to warn him of my return.

My mind blanked, and all I could find there was the truth. "I forgot the lost pet files, and I had to come back for them."

He swore again with a bit more force. "And you decided to snoop where you don't belong."

It wasn't a question. It was a statement of fact.

My heart had crawled up into my throat now and lodged there. If he'd been the one to kill Paul, I'd be next. Hopefully pentobarbital was quick and painless the way everyone claimed.

I had to play the cards I had like they were the ones I wanted and hope my bluff would be enough. I opened my mouth to tell him that I was an undercover police officer sent here to investigate Paul's death, and that he didn't want to do anything stupid because I'd already called for back-up.

Instead I snapped my mouth back shut. His face had a panicked flush to it rather than an angry flush— white under the red rather than pure crimson.

I climbed to my feet. If he was scared, then I should advance. "What were you doing out there? I saw you take the dog you said you had to euthanize."

Craig's stretched out a hand toward me in a give-me-a-chance-to-explain gesture. "What I'm doing," he pointed back at the door, "is a good thing."

He inched toward me. My skin crawled, begging me to step back. His demeanor was such a switch from the egomaniacal Craig of earlier that a little voice whispered in the back of my mind that it could be a trick. He wanted to bring down my defenses so he could overpower me more easily.

"How so?" I asked.

"Paul was small-minded and couldn't see past his prejudices." He practically spit the words out. This hatred of Paul felt like the most genuine thing he'd said since we met. "He couldn't see the potential in certain breeds of dogs."

"Keep talking." I did take a step back this time. If he decided to grab for me, I wanted enough warning to block and knee him in the groin. "I don't see how that explains why you're sneaking a dog out of the shelter and lying about it. I imagine that'd get you fired."

Fear flickered across his eyes, fast and gone. "Many of those dogs could live a full life with time and retraining. Paul disagreed, so I started faking the paperwork and finding them new homes."

I glanced sideways at the kennel where I'd returned the Great Dane puppy. Her first reaction to me was so different from how she'd been afterward. Very few dogs were born aggressive. Most became that way through mistreatment. They deserved a second chance.

When I'd been poking around investigating my Uncle Stan's death, Russ warned me I needed to be careful because I could accidentally end up hurting the reputation of good people who hadn't done anything wrong. The way Craig went about saving the dogs was technically wrong, but his reasons were good, which added an additional layer to it. Was *wrong* always wrong, or did the motive behind it sometimes make it right?

I took another step backward. Everything he'd told me also gave him motive for murdering Paul, more so if Paul found out and threatened to fire him.

"Please, Nicole." The words seemed to rip from Craig like this was his first time having to beg for anything. "Don't tell anyone. I can't lose this job."

I didn't need to tell Erik about this immediately. I could take the time to hunt for corroborating evidence. If Craig had killed Paul, he'd done it for a specific reason, and he wouldn't be out hunting other victims. Plus, if Craig was telling the truth about Paul, it would hurt Erik to hear that his friend wasn't the man he thought he was.

But just in case Craig was the killer, I wanted him to believe I was on his side and would keep his secret. "I won't tell anyone." I mentally added *for now.* "I think it's a good thing what you're doing."

And hopefully I was right that the killer wouldn't strike again in the meantime.

Chapter 11

As I trekked from my house to the snowshoe and ski rental shop the next morning, I wasn't sure whether I hurt more or less than I had the day before. My legs felt a bit better, but I had a residual headache from bonking my skull on the shelves and a bruise the size of a small dog on my backside that hurt whenever I sat down and whenever I walked from falling on my tush repeatedly. So basically the only time I didn't hurt was when I was standing perfectly still, which was when my headache raged the worst.

I'd tucked a bottle of ibuprofen into the coat of Uncle Stan's that I'd selected for today to replace the coat I'd torn the day before. This one was his church coat, a gray wool that reached to my knees. If it ever got wet, it might crush me.

I shook the snow off my hair and hung the coat on the rack by the door. It might have been my imagination, but I think even the coat rack groaned under the weight of it.

The employee behind the counter didn't even glance up. His gaze was glued to the newspaper spread out in front of him. His mouth hung open.

"Did you see this?" he said. He waved me over, still without actually making eye contact.

I stopped on the opposite side of the counter. The paper was this morning's edition of Fair Haven's weekly newspaper. A smiling picture of Paul stared back at me from above the fold.

The employee slowly shook his head. "I can't believe it. I saw him just the day before. He came in and rented a pair of snowshoes." He glanced up and did a double-take. "You're not Russ."

Now that I had a clearer view of him, he looked to be in his mid-twenties, with the build of a lean athlete, maybe a runner, given his lanky proportions.

He slid off the stool he'd been perched on. "Are you here to rent something?"

"I'm Nicole. Stan was my uncle. Russ said you'd be teaching me about the shop today."

"Right. I'm Dave." He brushed off his hands on his jeans even though he hadn't been doing anything that would make them dirty and moved around to the front of the desk. His movements reminded me a bit of a praying mantis, his arms swinging with his movements. "Sorry about that. I just wasn't expecting someone so..." His mouth opened and closed.

After being judged as inept and stupid recently, maybe I didn't want to know what he'd expected and how I didn't fit it. But I'd rather know than assume incorrectly. If I'd been able to quirk an eyebrow at him, I would have done it. "So...?"

He swallowed hard. "Pretty."

"Oh." Heat filled my face. That was about as far as it could get from what I'd expected. "Well, thank you." I shifted my weight from one foot to the other until I could almost hear my mother tell me to stop squirming. "So how do things work around here?"

That seemed to snap him out of his awkward gawking. He walked me through the process of fitting people for snowshoes or skies, including making me take off my boots so he could demonstrate what a too big or too small fit felt like.

He put the final sample ski boot back on the shelf and shuffled a foot back and forth. "That's really about it until you can practice on a real person. I mean, there's repairing and stuff, but that takes years to learn."

I looked around the currently empty shop. "So what do you do when no one's here?"

"I clean the gear mostly." He shrugged and then his face lit up. "When I run out of stuff to do, though, I work on my novel."

Before I had a chance to answer, he strode back to the counter and pulled a notebook and pen out from beneath. "I've been plotting out an espionage novel, kind of like James Bond but with a CIA agent as the main character, but now"—he tapped his pen on the newspaper next to the image of Paul's face—"I'm thinking maybe I should write a mystery instead. You got to draw inspiration from real life if you want to write a great book."

I pulled a stool around to the opposite side of the counter so that I didn't have to sit next to him. After the *pretty* comment and how much time he'd spent touching my feet, this association was already awkward enough. And I was technically his boss. "Did you know Paul well?"

I guessed not from his lack of grief, but it was worth a shot.

He shook his head absently, already flipping through the pages of his notebook. "No more than I know any of our regulars, unless you count his shoe size." He clicked the end of the pen against his lower lip. "Unless I want to make this a sci-fi instead, alien abduction and experimentation probably won't work for how he died and who killed him."

Since it didn't seem like a customer was going to come in any time soon, maybe I should roll with it. Fair

Haven was a small town with an active gossip mill, after all. Who knew what useful information Dave might have holed up in his brain.

I propped my elbows up on the counter. "You said writers should draw inspiration from real life, so what do you think was the most likely motive for Paul's death?"

Dave had the pen cap between his teeth now. "He seemed like a nice guy the times I talked to him, and he wasn't married, so it couldn't have been jealousy or anything like that." His face lit up. "My sister works at the bank, though, and when she saw the paper this morning, she said she bet it had something to do with the large bank drafts he drew every month."

I'd bet that was the type of information his sister wasn't supposed to share with anyone. Every bank I'd ever used had a confidentiality policy. It wasn't something I could look in to on my own either, but Erik could. I'd never used a bank draft myself, but they probably had to be made out to someone and that meant the bank would have a record. "Did she say how much the bank drafts were for or who they were made out to?"

Dave was hunched over his notebook, scribbling madly. "Yeah, that's good. It had to be the person he was giving the money too. Maybe he had gambling debts. Or he was being blackmailed."

Apparently I'd lost him to his story. He wasn't really listening to me anymore. I wandered into the break room and made a pot of coffee. By the time it was ready, customers had started to filter in.

By noon, I'd learned everything I was going to about this part of the business. If I cut out early, I could call Erik and recommend that they look into Paul's financials if they hadn't already. I'd keep quiet on what I'd found out about Craig for now. If it turned out that Paul had some other situation going on that led to his death, there wasn't any need to drag Craig into the investigation, even if it would be nice to see his cockiness brought down a notch.

I told Dave I was taking off and thanked him for helping me, then shrugged back into Uncle Stan's ten-ton coat and headed for the door.

"Hey Nicole?"

I looked back over my shoulder at Dave. He passed his pen back and forth between his hands like he was nervous.

Oh good lord, he wasn't going to ask me out, was he? If he did, at least I could use the excuse that I shouldn't be dating my employees.

He held up his notebook. "Thanks for showing interest in my writing. Not a lot of people do."

I held back a cringe. Great. Now I felt like a total jerk, and a self-centered one at that. But I wasn't about to burst his bubble. I knew what it was like to feel as if no one cared about what you wanted to do with your life. "My pleasure. If that's your dream, don't let anyone talk you out of it, okay?"

He grinned. "Okay."

I ducked out the door while I had the chance and pulled out my cell phone. The question was, did I tell Erik over the phone or suggest we meet up? If we met, I might be able to find a way to let him know there wasn't anything going on between Mark and me. Right now, he might think I wasn't interested in going out again, but I'd be much better off dating him than mooning over a married man.

Then again, he also could have found someone else he'd rather date while I was away, and suggesting we meet up would put him in an awkward position.

Grrr. Dating was stupid. It was times like this that I saw the merit in arranged marriages. For other people at least. The last thing I'd have wanted was my parents choosing my husband for me.

I'd call, and if he blew me off, then I'd know.

He picked up on the second ring.

"Hey," I shifted my phone to the other hand, "I found a few things I thought you might want to know. Do you have time to get together today?"

The silence stretched a longer than it should have if he was only thinking through his schedule.

I wasn't going to force him to say he wasn't interested. "Or I can just tell you over the phone if that'd be more convenient."

"No, that's okay." His response was a bit too quick this time, as if he'd picked up on the vulnerability that'd snuck into my voice before I could stop it. "How about coffee? You haven't been to The Burnt Toast yet, have you? They make a pretty decent cup."

We agreed to meet in twenty minutes. Since he didn't offer to pick me up, I called Russ. He couldn't get away, but he told me where to find the spare keys for his truck. I wasn't brave enough to tell him I'd never driven anything bigger than my car before.

It took me three tries to parallel park in front of The Burnt Toast Café.

I tromped in, knocking the snow off my boots before stepping inside. Erik was at a table near the door.

He rose to his feet and his gaze flickered over Uncle Stan's coat. He held a garment bag out to me. "I guess it's a good thing I brought this back for you. I had it dry cleaned."

I accepted the bag and peeled the zipper down to peek inside. My coat. I zipped it back up instead of swapping it for Uncle Stan's. Maybe it was time for a new one.

Erik already had a coffee. That was about as clear as it could get. This wasn't a date. He wouldn't be buying my drink as well. And another date wouldn't be happening.

A waitress came over and took my order. I asked for it in a to-go cup. Erik didn't owe me anything. We hadn't even kissed. And if he'd figured out that he wasn't interested, it was actually honorable of him to stop now.

That left my dating prospects back to nil and took away the buffer he'd provided between my emotions and Mark.

The coffee went bitter in my mouth. Had I only wanted to date Erik because I couldn't be with Mark? That wasn't fair of me if that was true. Erik deserved to be someone's first choice.

"I'm on duty," he said, dragging me back to the reason for our meeting, "so I can't stay long."

I swept my hand sideways in a no-worries move, as if I could wipe away the awkwardness of the situation as well. "This shouldn't take long."

In hindsight, I felt silly for pressuring him into meeting with me at all, but there was nothing I could do about it now. I filled him in on what Dave told me. By the time it was out, I felt downright stupid. It wasn't even a real lead. It was secondhand.

Erik sat without speaking for a beat too long. Then he cleared his throat.

I might not know him well, but I did know what that tic of his meant. Maybe it wasn't nothing after all.

"I'll look into it." His voice was too controlled and formal, like he didn't want me to read anything into his reaction. "Please don't pursue this particular avenue further."

Seriously? That was like putting a piece of bacon in front of a hungry dog. "Where do you think the money was going?"

He gave me a flat stare.

I moistened my lips and pulled my cup of coffee closer. Ouch. Okay. So much for working as a team on this.

Then again, we'd never been a team. I'd used his need for an informant to weasel my way into the investigation, and even now, my motives weren't entirely pure. If Paul had been involved in something nefarious unrelated to the shelter, I could keep Craig's secret and the aggressive dogs could continue to get a fresh start they otherwise might not get. I needed to know whether the money led to Paul's killer or not.

Erik was already on his feet. "Thanks for your help. If you find out anything else—"

"I'll let you know."

My tone came out sharper than I intended, but I'd received the *concerned citizen blockade* enough from former Chief Wilson during the investigation of Uncle Stan's death. I hadn't expected it from Erik now.

Something had definitely changed between us.

We paid our bills—separately—and he strode out.

I might have stomped my feet a bit more than necessary as I exited the café. I clambered up into Russ' truck, and then waited for Erik's police cruiser and another car to pass me. I pulled out behind them.

When we reached the first intersection, he signaled and turned in the opposite direction of the police station.

What the heck? Hadn't he just said he needed to get back to work?

Erik wasn't a liar, not even to spare someone's feelings. An omission was the same as a lie in his mind. So what was going on here?

If I followed him, the worst that would happen is I'd waste a little time. I made a snap decision and turned in the same direction.

Tailing someone wasn't part of the curriculum at law school, and my parents had people for that any time they'd wanted someone followed. On TV, though, the important part was to keep far enough back to not arouse suspicion.

Erik headed out of Fair Haven.

I did an air punch. No way was this official business. His jurisdiction ended at the city limits.

My arm sank down, the joy gone from the punch. If this wasn't official business, then I could think of only two reasons why he might be headed out of town. Either he was going for a mid-day tryst with whatever woman had taken my place or he was a part of whatever shady dealings had gotten Paul killed.

Chapter 12

A headache bloomed behind my eyes. Erik couldn't be involved in anything shady. If it turned out he was, I was never going to be able to trust another law enforcement officer—or another man—again. The only truly good and decent man in my life up until this point had been my Uncle Stan, and he'd been killed for it. Even Mark, for all the qualities that attracted me to him, was still a married man who had a highly questionable friendship with a woman who wasn't his wife.

No, whatever Erik was up to had to be above board. He'd asked me to help him find out information about Paul's relationships with the other workers at the shelter, after all. He didn't need to do that, and he'd have no reason to allow me into the investigation if he had something to hide.

My cell phone rang from my purse and I jerked. The truck swerved slightly.

I straightened out. Russ' truck wasn't Bluetooth-equipped, so I slowed my speed and fished it out. "This is Nicole."

"Why are you following me, Nicole?"

Crap. I stank at covert surveillance. "How did you know?"

"I'm a police officer." There was a hint of amusement in his voice. "Besides, Russ' truck has a distinctive bend to the fender where they backed a tractor into it one spring while removing dead trees from the bush. It's hard to miss."

That made sense. Everybody new everybody else in this town, and Erik was trained to be observant.

"There's a gas station coming up," he said. "Pull the truck over."

I disconnected the call and slammed a palm into the steering wheel. He had every right to lecture me. I was a civilian poking my nose, once again, into an investigation. Even though he'd asked for my help, it'd been in a limited capacity, and I'd tried to push beyond that.

I pulled into the empty parking space next to Erik's cruiser in the gas station lot. He was already out of his car, leaning against the passenger side.

I rolled down my window. "I promise not to follow you anymore."

He stepped away from the vehicle, pulled open the passenger side door, and hooked a thumb toward it. "If you're quick, I won't make you sit in the back."

He couldn't arrest me for following him, so... "Are you inviting me to ride along?"

His face remained expressionless, and he tilted his head slightly toward the open door.

I clambered out of the truck, locked it, and climbed in before he could change his mind. This trip must be about the case after all.

When we were back out on the road, he glanced sidelong at me. "I hope you didn't have any other plans for this afternoon. We've got a long drive ahead of us."

I texted Russ so he wouldn't worry—and so he'd know where his truck was if he wanted to pick it up. "Who do you think he was paying?"

"Could we talk about something else on the way? If I'm right about where the money was going, this is going to be a hard visit."

My innate curiosity sprinted around inside of me like a hyperactive hamster on a wheel, but I locked it inside. This case was personal for me because I'd accidentally run into the victim, but for Erik, it was more.

All my activities in the past few days had revolved around learning more about Paul, so I couldn't even entertain Erik with the stories that otherwise might have brought a smile to his face—or at least as close to a smile as the man ever came. Truth be told, I didn't feel much like putting in that work anyway. It was a lot less fun to work on making someone else laugh than it was to naturally laugh together.

I defaulted to the safe option and asked him how he was finding the role of interim chief. The conversation took off from there and we spent the drive "talking shop" about where he hoped his career would head and what I hoped to be able to do at Sugarwood.

Finally, Erik stopped the car in front of a little house with white siding and a bike in the driveway.

He went still and his jaw stiffened. "Wait here for a minute. I'll come back for you."

A little feeling like I didn't belong here wiggled along the back of my neck, but there wasn't anything I could do about it now. I'd made such a fuss about coming. "I'll wait."

Erik squared his shoulders and left the car. A woman with brown hair in a pixie cut, wearing a pixelated green uniform that looked like it belonged to some branch of the military, opened the door. Her face broke into a smile and she threw her arms around Erik's neck.

I didn't feel a twinge of jealousy. Shouldn't I feel something over the fact that he wasn't interested in me anymore and he was hugging someone else?

Erik said something and the smile faded from the woman's face. They went inside. I started a game of Sudoku, insanity-level difficulty, on my phone to distract myself and to keep from thinking too much about why I didn't have a green-eyed monster dancing a jig on my shoulder.

It was fifteen to twenty minutes before Erik came back out. He waved to me from the porch, and I joined him. His face was grim, and my stomach hollowed out even more. The way Erik acted made the situation feel different somehow. Personal.

The fatigues-clad woman waited for us in the living room. Her eyes were puffed and red, like the last fifteen minutes had been spent crying. People could fake tears, but these didn't look pretend to me. It blew my theory of blackmail away. No blackmailer cared like that for the person they were extorting money from.

She offered me her hand. "Captain Melissa Goering, U.S. Marine Corps."

Her handshake was solid. I returned an equally firm grip. "Nicole Fitzhenry-Dawes."

"You're not a police officer," Melissa said.

I glanced down at my man-sized jacket. "No, I'm a..." What was I anymore? Maple syrup farmer? Part-time animal shelter employee? Neither of those explained why I was part of the investigation, and I didn't want to put Erik in a bad position since he obviously hadn't gone into detail about why I was here. "I'm a lawyer."

She nodded her head. I hadn't claimed I was the prosecuting attorney on Paul's case, but that's likely what she assumed.

Melissa gestured to the couch. "Please take a seat. Erik said you both have some questions about Paul."

Erik had moved over to the nearest wall to stand in front of a line of three pictures. The one I could see around him showed Melissa with a blond-haired little boy, maybe five or six years old. It might be a nephew, but based on the bike in the front yard, I'd guess son.

The pieces weren't coming together for me. Erik thought this woman connected to Paul's secretive bank withdrawals, but she hardly looked like a drug dealer or like she needed anyone's charity.

Erik turned away from the photos. With him out of the way, I had a clear view of the remaining two. One showed Melissa, the little boy, and two older people. The woman had the same facial structure and smile, so I'd guess they were her parents. The other was of about a dozen or so Marines in dress uniforms. I couldn't make out faces from this distance, but the woman in the skirt was likely Melissa. One of the men standing next to her was built like Erik. That might explain how they knew each other, but it didn't explain what we were doing here.

Erik selected a spot on the opposite end of the couch. "We'll keep this as quick as possible so we can be done before Jacob comes home from school."

Melissa perched on the arm of the chair across from us, her back straight in that unnaturally erect way the military trained into its members. It made her look strong and confident even though she clutched a shredded tissue in her hand.

"I'd appreciate that," she said. "This news is going to be hard enough for him."

Erik cleared his throat. "Jacob is Paul's son, isn't he?"

Melissa's shoulders lost their straight line for a second and her gaze dropped to the ground. Then she pulled everything back into place and gave Erik a defiant look. "Yes."

I stayed quiet, giving myself time to work it through in my mind. The money must have been child support, except that wasn't something most people felt the need to hide. And why didn't Erik know that one of his closest friends had a son?

I glanced in Erik's direction, and the pictures on the wall behind him caught my gaze again. Hadn't Erik said he and Paul served together? If that was Erik in the photo with Melissa, then they all served together. I didn't know how long Erik and Paul had been out but...

"Your son was conceived while you were serving together?"

Melissa's gaze shifted to Erik. "I'm sorry we didn't tell you," she said, her voice soft. "It wasn't that we didn't trust you. At first we wanted to protect you from having to lie for us, and then so much time passed that we didn't know how to say something."

"You did what you felt you had to do. When you had Jacob, I knew the father had to be someone in our unit. The timing." Erik's Adam's apple worked up and down in his throat. "I should have put the clues together sooner. I wondered why Paul moved up here instead of south the way he planned after he got out. He always hated everything to do with winter."

Tears slid down Melissa's cheeks. She didn't try to hide them. She just let them fall like a badge of honor, and maybe they were. "It was for us. When I got assigned here, he wanted to be within driving distance so he could see us as often as possible."

My throat tightened, and as selfish as it was, all I could think was how grateful I was that I hadn't been the one to kill Paul, even accidentally, and cause all this grief. "Why did you need to keep it a secret?" I asked.

To their credit, neither of them looked at me like a stupid civilian. Erik gave Melissa an it's-your-story-to-tell nod.

She wiped her nose. "The military has certain rules about fraternization. To prevent someone from abusing their power or losing objectivity, officers are prohibited from having any sort of a relationship with the personnel serving under them."

That explained why they'd hidden it when they were both still serving. "But Paul's been out for a while. Could they have still done something to him post-discharge for sleeping with a subordinate while he was serving?"

Erik and Melissa exchanged a quick glance.

Erik angled toward me. "Melissa was our ranking officer. Paul was her subordinate."

I bit down on the inside of my cheek. Talk about making a gender-biased assumption. Of all people, I should know that a woman could lead capably—look at my mother, after all. She was one of the top criminal defense attorneys in the country, right alongside my dad. "I shouldn't have assumed. I'm sorry."

Melissa shrugged. "You get used to it after a while."

"You shouldn't have to, and especially not from another woman." I wasn't going to make any more assumptions in this case. I was going to ask to be certain. "So you were still hiding your relationship because you were worried about the repercussions for your career?"

"We'd been talking lately about whether it was finally safe for us to openly be together given how much time had passed. But I'm up for a promotion, and we thought why not wait a few months longer." Melissa yanked another handful of tissues from the box. "Now I wish we hadn't wasted all these years. If I had it to do over again—"

Her voice broke and she waved her hand in front of her. It was okay. I didn't need her to say any more when every word about what could have been would only hurt her more.

I rose to my feet. "I'm sorry to have intruded on you at a time like this."

Melissa simply nodded.

Erik went to her side and rested a hand on her shoulder. "You need anything, you call me. I don't know if Paul had a will, but if he didn't, let me know. I'll make sure we figure out whatever needs to be done to prove Jacob's his son so he can inherit."

I motioned to Erik that I'd wait in the car.

Today hadn't gone at all the way I'd imagined. Melissa hadn't killed Paul, and so all fingers pointed back to Craig. Unfortunately, I wanted to tell Erik about Craig's story even less now than I had before. My impartiality vanished the moment I realized that money had been going to support his family.

I wanted him to be as good a man as Erik and Melissa believed him to be. I wanted them to be able to grieve him without any reservations or black marks on their memories. After the circumstances surrounding Uncle Stan's death and the situation surrounding my ex-boyfriend, I knew what it felt like to think the person you'd loved and trusted wasn't who you thought they were. Your whole world suddenly felt more like a mirage than reality, and you started to question everything—your other relationships, your judgment, yourself.

I wouldn't do that to them without more evidence that Craig was telling the truth. Once I found it, I'd have no choice but to tell Erik. Because if Craig was telling the truth about Paul's prejudice against certain breeds of dog and about how Craig was attempting to counteract that, then Craig had a strong motive for

killing Paul. Even if Paul hadn't found out and threatened to fire him, Craig might have been angry enough
at what Paul was doing to kill him. People had killed
over a lot less.

Chapter 13

By the time Erik climbed back into the car, the sky had taken on the dusky tones that signaled the impending sunset. We headed back for Fair Haven.

I stifled a yawn. The past few days had been draining, both emotionally and physically. Tomorrow I was back at the shelter. Since it was Sunday, I was the only one scheduled—Craig crossed off Paul's name and wrote mine in—and I only needed to stop in for feeding and cleaning. That meant I'd have a few hours to rest and attend the lost pets meeting tomorrow afternoon. Bonnie had followed through on her promise and called a few people she thought would be interested.

Another yawn torqued my jaw. I shifted in the seat so that I could see Erik without wrenching my neck. "Thank you. For bringing me along. I know you don't owe me any information about the case, and I'm sure that would have been easier without me."

He opened his mouth as if he were about the reply, then closed it again.

The silence stretched, making my brain itch. The urge to fill it built inside me, filling up every corner with words I wanted to say simply so there was some sound in the car other than our breathing, the whoosh of air from the heater, and the friction of the tires on the asphalt.

"I've always been too curious. Nosy, my Uncle Stan used to call it. When I was a kid, I couldn't even wait for my birthday or Christmas to know what my presents were. I'd hunt for them until I found them."

His gaze slid sideways toward me with that enigmatic expression on his face.

My cheeks warmed. "It's not my best quality."

"It's not a bad quality either. Under the right circumstances." Erik sighed and scrubbed a hand over his head. "I owe you an apology as well."

It was like watching the end of a TV show when I'd missed the beginning. "What could you possibly owe me an apology for?"

"I wasn't keeping you out of the loop because you're a civilian. I closed you out because..." He grimaced like talking about this was physically painful. "I was letting personal reactions...I lost my objectivity."

Part of me wanted to let it go at that. Seeing him uncomfortable made me want to squirm. But I had a sense that if we didn't talk about whatever this was now, we'd lose any chance of a friendship going forward. Our truncated meeting at The Burnt Toast this morning had been borderline angry on both our parts.

"Lost your objectivity how?" In my mind, I ran back through everything that had happened since I'd returned to Fair Haven. Other than running over the body of his friend—which he hadn't seemed to hold a grudge about at the time—I couldn't think about anything I'd done to insult or harm him. That didn't mean I hadn't. "If I did something to upset you, it wasn't intentional, and I'd like a chance to make it right."

He ran a finger under his uniform collar as if he wished he could loosen it off a bit. "When I asked you out, you could have just told me you were interested in someone else."

Only my mom's voice in my head telling me not to let my mouth hang open, it'd catch flies, kept my lower jaw from bouncing off my chest.

He had to mean Mark, but I was *not* about to admit to being interested in a married man. "I don't know what you—"

His expression stopped the words on their way out. His look said *are you really trying to lie to a police officer?*

"It's not what you think," I finished lamely.

He shook his head. "It's exactly what I think. I saw how he looked at you, and I saw the way you looked back at him. That's not something brand-new. It had to have started during your first visit to Fair Haven."

What could I say in response to that?

That nothing had happened between Mark and me? It would be the truth, but he wasn't accusing me of actions—he was accusing me of feelings. Those I couldn't honestly deny. I already cared about Mark more than was appropriate.

I could say that it didn't matter because Mark was married, and I wasn't going to cross that line. But that was as good as saying I'd only gone out with Erik because I couldn't date Mark. He didn't need to hear it. It seemed like he already knew.

Which left me without an answer at all.

I buried my face in my hands. What a mess.

"Mark's a good man," Erik said.

I knew it. And I heard what Erik meant even if he didn't say it aloud.

A good man doesn't cheat on his wife. Mark wouldn't cheat on his wife. And I didn't want him to. I wouldn't respect him anymore if he did, and I wouldn't respect myself. I couldn't destroy another woman's happiness to try to snatch at my own.

The fact that Erik had said Mark was a good man rather than that Mark and his wife were separated answered another question for me. My last tendrils of hope slipped away.

I had no future with Mark.

I removed my hands from my face and turned to the window, watching the evergreen trees zip by in the distance, a green-blue blur against the white of the ground.

I had no future with Mark, and my feelings for him meant I also had no future with Erik. "You're a good man too," I said.

"But I'm not the right man for you."

No, he wasn't. And it was okay that Erik and I weren't right for each other. It didn't mean something was wrong with either of us. With me.

Uncle Stan used to say that everything happens for a reason. Maybe the reason I'd met Mark was to help me understand better what the right man for me would be like. And to understand that I wasn't going to be happy in a relationship if I dove into any opportunity that came along simply because a man was nice and was interested.

I stretched my hand out toward Erik without looking in his direction. A warm, calloused palm slid into mine and squeezed.

Tears threatened to clog my throat. I swallowed them down. Why did it feel like we were breaking up when we hadn't even been officially dating? "I know it's a cliché, but is there any chance we can still be friends?"

"I'd like to try."

My phone rang early the next morning while I was at the shelter, balancing a bowl of dog kibble in one hand and a full bowl of water in the other. Normally I would have let it go to voicemail, but I still hadn't heard back from the owner of the Great Dane puppy. With my luck, if I missed a call, it would be theirs and it'd be days before I could reach them again.

I slid the bowls down on top of the clothes dryer and wiggled my phone out of my back pocket. Mark's name flashed on the caller ID.

I moved to swipe the answer bar, but stopped a fraction of an inch over the screen. Talking, emailing, and texting him while I was back in DC made me care about him more, a lot more than a simple crush on a handsome man. I could still see Ahanti's eyebrows form skeptical triangles when I told her I could handle it and that I wouldn't allow myself to get carried away.

Seemed like the only one I was fooling with my lies was myself.

I shouldn't answer his call.

The problem was I'd promised to go with him to church this morning. I'd been so busy this week that we hadn't talked much, and since I'd wanted to check out my Uncle Stan's church, Mark invited me along. Now a war raged inside me. Wisdom pitted itself

against my mother's mantra about how rude and disre-
spectful it was to cancel plans on someone last minute.

The phone stopped ringing, but I continued staring
at the screen. I couldn't cut Mark off without talking to
him about it. Doing it over the phone would be easier
and slightly less embarrassing for me, but not fair to
him. I'd go with him to church and show him the Great
Dane puppy the way I promised. Then before we part-
ed today, I'd have to explain to him that I couldn't
spend time with him anymore.

Unless his wife was with him this time. I hadn't
considered that. Based on the fact that I hadn't met her
during my previous brief stay in Fair Haven, I'd
guessed that she traveled a lot for work. Fingers
crossed she was gone on another trip. If I waited, I
might well lose my courage.

I slid the dishes into the kennel of a scraggly brown
dog who always looked like he was grinning at me and
pushed redial on my phone.

"I'm about five minutes out," Mark said. "I thought
you might like a warning call so you'd have time to finish up."

Smiley dog had been the last one, so I spent the rest
of my time until Mark arrived playing with the Dane
puppy. If I were her owner, I wouldn't have waited
even an hour to return the call and pick her up.

Maybe they didn't want her anymore and she'd be
adoptable. With my life path, I could set my own hours
now. I could have a dog. And a cat.

I called their number again and left another message.

A knock sounded on the front door. I kissed the puppy on the head, tucked her back into her kennel, and met Mark.

The sermon left me with questions. In my fervor to have Mark answer them, I forgot I was supposed to be spending less time with him and instead we ended up out to lunch.

The waitress' dirty look when she brought the bill, like I was corrupting Fair Haven's favorite son, jerked me back to my senses.

I glanced at my watch. I was due at the lost pets meeting in 15 minutes anyway, which gave me no time to talk to Mark the way I'd planned, but a perfect excuse to slip away.

Chicken, a voice inside my head said.

If it wouldn't have been classified as talking to myself, I would have told it to shut up.

I dragged the bill toward me. "I've got to get going, so let me see what my half is."

Mark clamped a hand over mine. A tingle shot up my arm, and my mouth went dry. Oh dear Lord I was in so much trouble where this man was concerned.

He flashed me his dimples. "My treat."

My tongue dissolved into the bottom of my mouth. I nodded and wriggled my hand out from under his.

He handed the waitress his credit card. She glared at me as she walked away. If looks could kill, I'd have been laid out on Mark's cadaver table already.

He seemed completely oblivious.

He signed the slip she brought and handed it back to her, then helped me slide into Uncle Stan's gargantuan wool coat. I'd tried putting mine on this morning, but I took it right back off again.

We climbed into Mark's truck and he started the engine. "Where to, m'lady?" he asked in a corny British accent.

"Elm Street, Jeeves." I attempted my own British accent, but I ended up sounding like I'd been to the dentist and still had cotton balls stuffed in my cheeks.

"Accents aren't your thing, are they?"

My cheeks hurt from the smile stretching across them. "Not so much. I'm great at funny faces though."

"I'll keep that in mind for the future."

So much for telling him you can't spend time with him anymore, the annoying voice of my conscience said.

Mark was my kryptonite.

I was going to have to do it. Even if the timing was terrible. No time was going to be good for a conversation where you had to tell your closet friend in town that you couldn't see him anymore because you were an idiot who had no more control over her emotions than a hormonal teenager.

"What's at Elm Street?" he asked before I could pull my thoughts together.

I rolled my eyes. "Long story." I filled him in as we drove.

"I guess that means we don't have time to swing by the shelter and meet this puppy you're in love with."

"I am falling in love with the puppy." *Only the puppy?* the accusing voice asked. This time I did mentally tell it to shut up. "But we can't stop now. Not if I don't want to be late. I lost track of time."

He got a little-boy grin on his face like I'd given him a compliment. "I don't have anything else to do today. I might as well go to the meeting with you, and then we can swing by the shelter after."

My mind ground to a halt. There had to be a convincing reason why we couldn't spend the rest of the day together. Aaaand...I had nothing. "Won't you be bored?" Talk about grasping at straws.

He shook his head. "I usually volunteer when the shelter has a fundraiser. I'd like helping with this new group."

My first though was *aww*. My second was *crap*.

We pulled into Bonnie's driveway. Mark had the truck turned off and was headed for the door before I could think up any other plausible reason for him to leave. I hoisted my soft-sided briefcase over my shoulder and followed him.

Bonnie threw open the door and sucked me into another of her bone-crushing hugs. My cheek plastered up against her apple-blossom-bedecked dress. "I was so excited last night that I couldn't—"

Her arms dropped away and I stumbled back, unprepared for the sudden release.

"And you brought a handsome friend." She squinted her eyes. "One of the Cavanaugh boys. Mark?"

He bobbed his head. "Hello, Miss. Bonnie."

He offered his hand, but she pulled him into a hug as well.

"It's been so many years." She let him go and turned to me. "I used to clean for the funeral home back before my knees gave out, and I watched those three boys grow up playing and doing homework around the dead bodies. No wonder they all turned to working with dead people once they grew up."

I'd almost forgotten Mark had once mentioned a younger brother who worked as a homicide detective in Detroit. They *had* all turned to careers involving corpses.

She waved us inside. We left our shoes in the entryway pile.

As we moved through the hallway, Mark tilted his head down toward mine and nodded at my feet. "No monkey socks today?"

Heat flared in my belly. It had to be from embarrassment rather than from how close his face was to mine. "I learned my lesson about you Northerners and removing your shoes. I left all the silly socks at home today."

"Too bad."

I nearly tripped over my own feet. I shifted my gaze to the photos lining Bonnie's wall to distract myself from Mark's closeness and the way he was smiling at me. If he hadn't been a married man, I might have described the look as smitten.

Where most people would have displayed family photos, Bonnie had pictures of Toby. Toby "opening" a present at Christmas. Toby dressed up as a pumpkin for Halloween. Toby wearing a tuxedo vest and standing next to Bonnie in a fancy dress.

Five other people waited in her living room—one man and four women—ranging in age from around eighteen to sixty. One woman bounced a baby on her knee.

Bonnie motioned us to the last empty spots, a love seat. I sat and shifted close to one arm, trying to make sure there was plenty of room for Mark without us touching. As soon as he sat down, the middle of the couch bowed slightly and tilted me sideways into him.

I was not going to be able to concentrate if I had to sit crushed up against him. I shot back to my feet.

Bonnie waved me forward as if she'd planned all along for me to address the group from the front of the room where a TV not much larger than a cereal box perched on a stand. "This is Nicole from the shelter, and she's generously offered to lead this group."

The woman who looked to be near sixty started to clap, but it fizzled away when no one else joined her.

The only way this afternoon could get more uncomfortable was if I leaned over and ripped my pants or if my speaking-in-a-crowded-courtroom stutter decided this group was close enough and resurrected itself. Flutters built in my stomach and rose up into my throat like bubbles.

I could do this. I was a grownup. Grownups sometimes had to talk to more than one person at once.

I plowed through my idea about setting up a Facebook group where people could post pictures of their lost pets and also pictures of animals they found or who were brought into the shelter.

"And I'm going to talk to the local vet clinic about running a microchip clinic." I dug into the bag and pulled out a couple of the file folders. "But I think the first thing we should do is divide up these files and look into which animals are still missing and which have been found."

The group burst into a flurry of talk about who would run the Facebook group and what to name it.

I flipped open the first file folder. I hadn't had time to actually look through them the way I'd planned, but it seemed like Paul organized them based on animal and color. An efficient system since that's all they'd know about any animal brought in.

I handed each person a folder and sat back beside Mark. The couch cushion shifted again, but I was prepared this time and kept myself from sliding into him.

I gave him one of the remaining folders. "You did say you wanted to help, right?" I whispered.

He nudged my shoulder with his and I had to grab the arm of the love seat to keep from tumbling into him. I clamped my lips together to keep from sticking my tongue out at him.

I slid the final folder out for myself and flipped through it. Instead of being arranged by animal and color the way the others were, mine seemed to be all large-breed dogs or breeds with a reputation for aggression. I turned the pages more slowly. Rottweilers, Mastiffs, Dobermans, Pitbulls, German Shepherds...why had these been taken out of the normal files?

Craig's accusations of Paul's prejudice flooded back into my mind. I gnawed on the inside of my cheek. Maybe these were simply pets who'd already been found. I turned another page and the heavily-jowled face of Bonnie's Toby stared back at me. So much for that theory.

"Bruno's not in the file," the young mom with the baby on her knee said. "But I know I took a lost-pet flier to the shelter for them to keep in case he showed up there."

Bonnie's forehead had wrinkled into layers that bore a frightening resemblance to Toby's folds of skin. She was leaning toward the armchair of the teenage girl and looking at the fliers in the girl's folder. "Toby's not in this one, either." She huffed and her ample bosom bounced rapidly like she might be beginning to hyperventilate. "This is why I kept making Paul take me into the back kennel so I could look for myself. I knew we couldn't trust him to keep watch for them."

I wrapped my fingers around Toby's page in my file to show her that he had kept Toby on file as a lost pet, but then I flattened my palm over the picture. If I handed this to her, she might ask about my folder. Anyone would quickly notice what I had—for some reason, Paul had isolated these dogs from the rest of the records.

The couch cushion under me shifted again. I glanced up. Mark's gaze was focused on the folder in my hands, and a small crinkle formed between his eyes. Beneath where I'd put my hand to cover Toby's picture, Bonnie's name and phone number were still clearly visible.

I snapped the folder closed. "I might have left some records behind without realizing it, or Toby and Bruno might have been accidentally slipped into another file. That's why I think it's so important for us to go through all these records."

Bonnie nodded her head, and her breathing eased. "Well then, how about we pick the date and time for our next meeting, and then have some snacks."

I tucked my folder back into my bag. "I have to get back to the shelter for the evening feeding and cleaning. Could you call me with the details?"

Bonnie agreed to let me know what they selected, then she bustled into the kitchen. Before we had our shoes on, she returned with a plastic container filled with cookies and squares.

She pressed the container into my hands. "When I found out you were Stan Dawes' niece, I whipped up a batch of my maple syrup fudge and my maple syrup cookies in his honor. I couldn't let you leave without taking a few home with you."

Tears pressed at the corners of my eyes. Enough time had passed since Uncle Stan's death that sometimes I could think about him without wanting to cry. Now wasn't one of those times.

"Thank you," I squeezed out.

For a second Bonnie looked like she was going to give me another hug, but my arms were full of sweets and my briefcase bag.

She waved her hands at us instead. "Off with you, then. Go take care of those needy animals."

As soon as Mark had us back on the road, heading in the direction of the shelter, I slumped back in his seat. I had more evidence now as to who might have killed Paul and why, but it wasn't what I'd hoped for.

I popped the lid on the container of sweets and shoved a cookie into my mouth. It wasn't overly sweet the way I'd expected. Instead it was like a maple-flavored sugar cookie, soft on the inside and with a tiny crunch from the granulated sugar on the outside.

Unfortunately, as good as it was, it didn't solve my problem, not that my propensity to stress eat ever did.

"Okay," Mark said. "What's going on?"

What I'd seen at the shelter and Craig accusations poured out. "And now it looks like he'd set aside any reports of big dogs who were missing and he wasn't treating them the same way. He might have even been acting as a vigilante, getting rid of dogs in the city that he saw as potential threats to public safety."

Mark reached over and tucked my hair behind my ear. I sucked in a little breath and prayed he didn't notice. His innocent touches were going to be the death of me.

"I know you want to protect the dogs Craig might have saved, but you need to tell Erik. And I don't think you should work with Craig alone again until we know if he was involved or not."

I nibbled another cookie. He was right. Spending time alone, even in the daylight, with a man who might be a murderer wasn't smart. Still, my stomach twisted itself up like a Twizzler at the thought of having to tell Erik that Paul might not have been the good guy he thought he was. "He and Erik were so close..."

Mark shook his head emphatically. "Erik won't let that influence him. He'll investigate the case the same as if he didn't know the victim."

"That's not what I mean." I eyed the remainder of the fudge and cookies, but snapped the top in place. I'd already need another day out on snowshoes to burn off what I'd eaten. "It'll hurt him if Paul was really doing what Craig said."

"Oh." Mark's hands twitched around the steering wheel and his knuckles turned white the same way they had when he thought I'd been flirting with Jason, the owner of Beaver's Tail Brewery. "I see."

I opened my mouth to tell him there wasn't anything but friendship between Erik and me, but I snapped my mouth shut instead. I needed distance from Mark, and letting him stew in his weird jealous fit might be the way to get it while avoiding an awkward conversation about my feelings.

That wasn't fair to Mark, but I wasn't sure I had the fortitude to cut off my friendship with him right now, not with my stomach already in a knot over the potential motive for Paul's murder.

I got out my phone. "I'll call him now." There was an edge to my voice. I winched and ducked my head forward so my hair hid my face.

Mark stopped the truck in the shelter parking lot.

Erik answered on the first ring and I repeated the same information that I'd given to Mark, including my theories.

I could hear Erik breathing, so I knew the call hadn't dropped, but he didn't respond at first.

A chair squeaked like he was shifting positions. "I'll pay a visit to Craig tonight. Are you scheduled to work at the shelter anytime soon?"

"I'm in the parking lot now for the night care, and I'm on again tomorrow morning by myself."

"I'd rather you weren't there alone in case Craig shows up unannounced and he did have something to do with Paul's death. Sit tight. I'll send someone else to question Craig, and I'll join you."

I glanced in Mark's direction. He stared out the driver's side window, hands still in a rock-crushing hold on the steering wheel. After his reaction to my concern for Erik, I wasn't sure if he still planned to come in and meet the puppy or not. It'd be better over-all if Mark left and Erik kept me company, but then Erik wouldn't be able to take part in the interview with Craig. He should be the one to do it.

I touched Mark's arm. He turned just his head.

Are you still coming in? I mouthed.

His shoulders came down away from his ears a touch, and he quirked an eyebrow at me. I took that as a *yes*.

If I kept my explanation to Erik vague enough, he might think I meant Russ was with me.

"I'm not alone," I said to Erik. "And he's willing to stay while I do what I need to here."

When I glanced up at Mark again, he'd let go of the steering wheel, but his lips formed a hard line. No sign of a dimple anywhere. I missed them already.

"Stay safe," Erik said.

"You too."

I disconnected the call, and left the baked goods and my briefcase in his truck since he'd have to give me a ride home after anyway. Mark and I walked toward the shelter door, at least two feet of space between us.

I unlocked the building, dropped Uncle Stan's coat on one of the waiting room chairs, and scurried away from Mark to the kennel area.

He caught up to me and laid a hand on my shoulder. My body froze, but my heart kicked up like a regular car running on high-octane gas.

He turned me around to face him, and his hand slid down to rest on my upper arm. "Why did you avoid telling Erik you were with me?"

I couldn't bring my gaze above his chest. My hands shook. I clenched them into fists.

I'd done everything I could to avoid this conversation, and it'd found me anyway. *The truth will set you free*, the pastor had said in this morning's sermon. "Erik has concerns about...our friendship."

Mark's hand clenched and released but didn't leave my arm. "Why does it matter what Erik thinks?"

Deep breath in. I could do this. I had to do this.

I stepped back, breaking the contact. A piece of me seemed to rip away and stay behind. It wasn't just that I was attracted to him. It was more. Next to Ahanti, Mark was the best friend I'd ever had.

That was exactly why I had to do this. If I continued to see him, my self-control and resolve would only hold out so long, and if he slipped as well, I'd be a willing adulteress this time.

My gaze was down to his shoes now, with their perfectly even laces. I was done with married men breaking my heart, intentionally or unintentionally. I wasn't going to waver now. The blood in my veins turned to steel. "I have concerns as well. I've been trying to find a way to tell you all day."

"All day." His voice wavered. The shoes moved back out of my narrow range of sight. "All day today."

I nodded.

"You should have said something sooner."

I didn't look up until I heard the front door chime signaling he was gone. I gasped in air. I hadn't realized I'd been holding my breath.

I'd done it. I should feel liberated and proud. All I felt was empty. And now I was here alone, exactly how Erik hadn't wanted.

I dialed Russ' number. "I'm at the shelter, and I don't think I should be here alone, could you come?" I said in one gulp when he answered.

"Are you okay?"

He didn't need to carry all my burdens and certainly not this one, which would only remind him of the people he'd lost and the consequences that could come with adultery. "Yeah. Erik's gone to talk to a suspect, and he doesn't want me here alone."

"On my way."

I hurried through the clean-up and feeding. By the time the front door chime rang again and Russ called out to let me know it was him, I was done except for the Great Dane puppy. I opened her kennel and she launched herself at me, wriggling.

It probably broke every rule the shelter had, but I was taking her home with me for the night. I needed comfort, and it was either going to be cute puppy or eating my way through everything even remotely sweet in my cupboards, including spoonfuls of straight brown sugar from the bag.

I clipped a leash onto her collar.

Russ came around the corner, carrying my briefcase and the container of goodies from Bonnie. "Mark asked me to give these to you. Did you know he was sitting outside?"

He hadn't left me here unprotected, despite what had happened.

The hairline crack in my heart broke wide open, and I had the uncomfortable feeling that this time it might not heal.

Chapter 14

Russ must have noticed my silence on the drive home, but he didn't push. I brought the puppy to bed with me and cried myself to sleep. She smelled a little musty, but I could fix that with a bath, and the way she rested her head on my arm put a balm on my stinging heart. Even though I knew I'd done the right thing, it didn't make it hurt any less.

Russ picked me up the next morning. I had a feeling he noticed my red nose and swollen eyes, but he stayed quiet about it in an Uncle Stan-like waiting-me-out way. Either that or female emotions made him uncomfortable. I didn't know Russ well enough yet to be sure which it was.

He dropped me at Quantum Mechanics for my car, and I drove on to the shelter by myself. The sky hunkered low to the ground, a misty grey. Snowflakes wove their way down.

I parked in front of the shelter next to a maroon SUV.

Craig's SUV.

I thunked my head back against the headrest. Forgetting that I wasn't supposed to be at the shelter with Craig alone started my day off only marginally better than yesterday ended. There was only one thing I could do.

I called Erik. The phone rang three times, and I was trying to decide whether to wait in my car until I could reach him or go inside anyway when he picked up.

"How did it go with Craig last night? I'm sitting outside the shelter, his car's here, and I'm not sure if I should go in."

"I thought you said you were the only one scheduled this morning."

He was right. Craig wasn't supposed to be in until noon. "That's what I thought, too." I checked the puppy in my backseat. She whimpered and squirmed against her safety harness. I'd been too upset last night to grab her any food, so she hadn't had breakfast yet. "What do I do? I have a hungry puppy in my backseat."

"I'm not even going to ask why there's a puppy in your car." A pause like Erik switched the phone to his other ear. "Go on in, but stay on the line with me.

Craig told me the same story he told you. Swore he didn't have anything to do with Paul's death, but he didn't care for him, either."

I flinched. That had to be hard for Erik to hear when he was missing his friend. "Do you think he killed Paul?"

"He's our best suspect right now."

I propped the phone between my ear and shoulder and helped the puppy from the car. "But you don't think I'm in danger anymore?"

"Not now that we've talked to him. If anything happened to you now, he'd be the obvious suspect."

"I appreciate you staying on the phone with me nonetheless since he wasn't supposed to be here yet." I tugged the shelter door open. At least Craig left it unlocked for me. "What'll happen with his job?" I kept my voice low in case Craig was working near the front.

Only the chairs and empty front desk met me in the lobby.

"That's up to the city council," Erik said. "What he did violates shelter policies, but it isn't illegal. I doubt they'll fire him since he's currently their most experienced shelter employee. It might ruin his chances of becoming manager, though. I heard they're looking for an outside replacement."

That was probably for the best even if Craig turned out to be innocent. "Maybe the new manager will be open to using his channels for reforming the problem dogs."

I didn't mean to imply *unlike Paul*, but it unintentionally hung in the air between us.

The puppy bounced along beside me like a mini Tigger. If her owners took much longer getting back to me, I was going to name her so I didn't have to keep calling her *the puppy*.

All the rooms along the hallway were empty. Craig must already be back feeding the animals.

I shucked Uncle Stan's coat into the closet and followed the line of kennels, looking down each row. "That's weird."

"What's weird?"

I jumped and nearly dropped the phone. I'd almost forgotten Erik was still on the other end. "Craig's not in the kennel area. He must be out back with one of the dogs."

"I want you to find him and see how he reacts to you before I hang up, so could you check?"

The puppy wove around my feet, and I scratched the top of her head. Her tail whipped back and forth at hyper-speed. I'd feed her super quick first. I scooped out a bowl of food and set it down.

A smear of red on the freezer caught my attention. Dark red.

I inched toward the freezer. It was one of the large chest versions, wider than it was long.

"Did you find Craig?" Erik asked.

I rested a palm on the freezer handle. That smear probably wasn't blood—canned dog and cat food came

in a range of sickening shades of brown—and if I called
Erik down here for nothing, I'd be pulling him away
from important work. Staying on the phone while I
hunted for Craig ate up enough of his time already.

I hauled in a steadying breath and threw open the
freezer lid.

Craig's lifeless eyes stared back at me, a bullet hole
between them.

Five minutes later, Erik slid into the passenger side
of my car. The first squad car arrived in three. By then
I was already huddled in my car with the Dane puppy
in my lap. I couldn't quite convince myself to stay inside, knowing Craig's frozen body was stuffed into the
freezer.

"I'll have one of my men feed and clean the animals," Erik said. "We can't have civilians inside until
we've released the scene."

I pressed two fingers into the space between my
eyes. For the first time since I'd decided to move to
Fair Haven, I wished I'd chosen to stay in DC. "This
has been the crappiest week ever."

"I'll have an officer drive you home as soon as I can
spare someone."

He didn't touch me the way he would have before
our conversation defining our relationship. In one way,
I appreciated him keeping the boundaries clear. In another way, I wanted someone to hug me so I could hide

in their arms for a few minutes and block out the world.

I clutched the puppy closer, and she rested her head over my shoulder. With Mark out of my life and Erik slotted into the friend zone, that was as close to a hug as I was going to get. "I guess Craig didn't kill Paul."

"Looks that way." Erik's gaze shifted to the side, looking out the window toward where the cruisers sat, and then back to me. "You're the only one who won't take this the wrong way because a man's dead. In a way, I'm relieved. It means Paul probably wasn't doing the things we were worried he was."

I did understand, and it was a relief that Craig's death meant Paul probably wasn't kidnapping and killing "dangerous" dogs.

Unfortunately, his death also meant the real killer was still on the loose, and now they'd taken two lives. But why kill Craig as well? All the theories I'd built crumbled if Craig wasn't the one who killed Paul.

I focused my attention back on Erik. Some friend I was. He'd been sharing and I hadn't been paying attention.

"I couldn't believe Paul would target certain dogs. He had a Saint Bernard growing up, and when he talked about what he wanted to do after his discharge, he considered becoming a police officer and joining a K9 unit. He hated animal cruelty of any kind."

That left us with more questions than answers once again, the biggest one being how Craig's and Paul's deaths were related, apart from them both being committed at the shelter.

Chapter 15

Despite a few skeptical glances, Erik didn't question me about taking the Dane puppy home with me. I guess he'd accepted that, with me, it was sometimes better not to know. Then he wouldn't have to try to stop me.

The officer I'd been entrusted to turned out to be Quincey Dornbush, and I convinced him to detour by Slugs, Snails, and Puppydog Tails, the local pet store, so I could buy puppy food. I also got her a purple collar and leash because the color looked pretty against her black and white spots. Besides, I had to have something to walk her with until I located her owner.

Another officer followed us home with my car.

Once I got her settled, I paced the length of the house. My fingers itched to pick up my phone and call Mark. Up until yesterday, that's exactly what I would have done. When I wasn't looking, he'd somehow become my first call whenever anything interesting happened.

I could call Ahanti or my mom instead, but Ahanti had a tendency to gloat when she was right, and I didn't need to hear a good-for-you about Mark. It felt anything but good right now. And my mom still believed that everything was negotiable, including marriage vows. It was amazing my parents had been faithfully and happily married for nearly thirty-five years considering their personalities and approach to life. Apart from that, if my mom found out I'd ended up in the middle of another murder investigation, she'd only ask why I couldn't have done that at home— meaning Virginia.

Maybe I didn't want to talk to anyone after all. Maybe what I needed was to be out in the peace of the woods.

I made sure the puppy would be okay for a couple of hours and called Russ. He assigned me another section of the sap lines to check, told me where the snowmobile keys were, and warned me to take a walkie-talkie with me. My phone might or might not work depending on where I went in the bush, and if I needed help, I'd want to be able to reach Dave back at the rental shop.

When I went into the shop for snowshoes, Dave flashed me a thousand-watt grin. "I decided on the motive for my mystery. It was a love triangle. It's always love, money, or revenge, right? Will you read a couple of pages once I've got something written?"

I agreed, tucked the map Russ had left for me into my utility belt, and hauled the rest of what I'd need out to the snowmobile. Russ had let me drive back the last time we went out, and his instructions came back to me easily.

I checked the tether and hit the ignition switch. Zipping across the fluffy snow, kicking it up in my wake, the drone of the machine, like a giant hornet, acted as white noise for my brain. I pushed the throttle further and the snowmobile responded. I'd never been able to outrun my problems on my bike, but now I had horsepower underneath me.

Unfortunately, once I stopped at the location marked on my map, they caught up to me.

I focused on tracing the powder blue sap lines back toward the main grounds. Not having Russ with me meant I had to mark my progress and go back for the snowmobile. The physical exertion felt good, though.

As I stopped the snowmobile at the second eighth of my allotted segment. Something about the snow to the left looked odd. I lifted my sunglasses and squinted against the glare of the sun off the snow. If Russ saw me doing it, he'd give me a lecture on snow blindness, but I didn't plan to leave them off long. I just wanted to see if the shadows played tricks on me.

I tramped in the direction of the spot. It was a depression like I'd seen the first time out, only much wider. Much too wide, in my opinion, to be a predator catching its prey, but I'd also never spent time in a bush before this week. The fresh snowfall covered the ground in a thick enough layer that any details of blood or footprints had long been covered over.

I hadn't shown Russ the original spot. This time I'd take a picture and check with him. Likely it was something natural and innocent, but he'd also said they'd had trouble in the past with teenagers breaking into the old sugar shack and fooling around. If this was more of the same, we'd need to decide whether it was a problem or not and what to do about it.

I stuffed my mittens in my pocket and dug out my phone. I snapped a photo and moved around the ring for a different angle. The phone rang in my hands.

I must be in one of the small pockets where I had a signal. Best not to move too far in either direction.

I flipped the phone around. The number looked vaguely familiar, but I couldn't place it.

"This is Nicole Fitzhenry-Dawes." Now that I wasn't a lawyer anymore, I could probably answer with my first name only, but old habits and all that.

"Is this the Nicole from Fair Haven Animal Shelter?" a woman's voice asked.

Little lightbulbs went on. This must be the puppy's owner. My chest tightened. I guess I wouldn't be keeping her after all. Hopefully her owner liked purple. "That's right. Are you calling about the Great Dane puppy?"

"I am, and I'm sorry it's taken me so long to return your call. My husband and I have been away on vacation."

I kicked at a clump of snow with my snowshoe, nearly lost my balance, and grabbed a tree branch. I couldn't even suggest they were negligent owners now. They had a legitimate reason for not returning my call. She might have even escaped from someone else while they were away.

"That's alright. We're closed today...for maintenance." A little white lie, but Craig's death hadn't been made public yet. I wasn't about to say there were police combing the shelter for evidence of a murder. And I didn't have the necessary paperwork to return her to them from my house. "I could meet you there tomorrow if you'd like."

"Well," the woman's voice suddenly sounded hesitant, "here's the thing. She disappeared almost a month ago now, and we thought she was gone for good. So we got another dog."

I frowned. The puppy only came in the day Paul died. Otherwise Craig would have seen her and logged her into the system. But that was just over a week ago. She was too young to survive on her own outside in the winter for the missing weeks. Despite her size, she was very much still a baby.

"We really can't have two dogs." Her voice sounded embarrassed now, like she'd misinterpreted my silence as censure.

Quite the opposite. The puppy could be mine now. "Don't worry. We'll find her a good and loving home." I could guarantee that. The timeline discrepancy still niggled at my mind like a sliver, though. "If you don't mind me asking, how did you lose her?"

"We didn't. Someone broke into our house. The police said the thief must have recognized her value and took her to re-sell. That's why we gave up and moved on almost immediately."

Maybe the dog-napper couldn't find someone to sell her to and set her loose instead, but Great Danes sold for over $1500. If it were me, I'd have waited longer than a couple of weeks to find a buyer for that kind of money.

"Thanks for returning my call," I said.

We disconnected, and I punched in Mark's number. He might have a fresh angle on this that I hadn't thought of.

I realized what I was doing before I tapped the button to dial. I canceled the call. He probably wouldn't have answered anyway.

My cell ringing woke me at 7:30 the next morning. I rolled over and grabbed the phone. My puppy—*my* puppy—grunted at me. I probably shouldn't let her keep sleeping in the bed with me. It was cute now while she weighed less than fifty pounds, but once she passed a hundred, it'd be like having a second person with me. A second person with doggie breath.

"Sorry to call so early," Erik said. "We'll be releasing the scene around noon and we've run into a problem."

Because we needed another problem. I shifted up to a sitting position and ran my tongue over my teeth. "What's that?"

"The shelter's now short-staffed and all the other workers are volunteers. Until the council's able to hire replacements..."

I moved my sleepy puppy to the floor and slid my feet into my slippers. "You need me to keep working there."

"Do you mind? It'd only be for another week at most."

I suppose I owed him for letting me poke into his murder investigation. "No problem. I'll take Craig's shift today, and then I'll look at the schedule and see if anyone else can come in a little extra."

I swung back by the pet store for toys, dishes, and a dog bed and was at the shelter by 2:30, giving the police extra time before I showed up. The police cars were gone and the yellow crime scene tape had been removed from the door.

I spent the next hour making calls to the volunteers and trying to fill the slots for the following week, then I pulled out a copy of the adoption form to fill in for my puppy.

The front door chime sounded. I brushed fur off my shirt, stepped over the puppy's sleeping body, and headed for the front.

The man in the waiting room looked up from his phone, and a jolt shot through my body.

It was the same man Craig had turned the aggressive dog over to.

Chapter 16

My heart beat so hard in my ears that I almost couldn't hear anything else. What was he doing here, coming through the front door? Given the clandestine nature of what he and Craig had been involved in, it didn't seem believable that they met openly, especially here. But maybe he didn't realize Craig was dead and he'd been trying to reach him.

I had to get a grip. This might be innocent. If it wasn't, I didn't want to broadcast more than I already had that I suspected anything.

You need to learn to control your emotions better, Nicole, my dad's taunting voice replayed in my head. *You let your opposition read you, and you'll lose.*

I plastered a smile on my face. I didn't have a Harry Potter Time-Turner, so the best I could do was cover.

"You surprised me," I said. "I thought you were my boyfriend. He was supposed to bring me a coffee, and he's late." I rolled my eyes. "He probably forgot again."

The man's return smile was buttery smooth and reminded me a bit of a professional poker player—definitely not an artsy type the way I'd originally thought, though a colorful tattoo did peek out from under his collar and up his neck.

He slid his phone back into his pocket. "I wouldn't hold it against him. Most of us don't do it on purpose."

My red-alert responses downgraded to yellow. Craig's death didn't mean he'd lied to me about why he'd been giving this man aggressive dogs. Craig's death also didn't mean that this man was dangerous or involved in the murders in any way. He might be a nice guy trying to do what he could to help animals in need of reconditioning. When I'd worked as a defense attorney, we poked holes in more than one case based on the prosecution presenting things as facts that could be coincidences. Jumping to unfounded conclusions would only give me an ulcer and lead me down rabbit trails that wouldn't solve this case.

"How can I help you?" I asked.

"I lost my dog, and I'm going around to shelters seeing if someone brought her in."

Still not condemning evidence, but that answer did feel a bit like trying to force together two puzzle pieces that didn't quite match. Would this man have a dog of his own apart from the dogs Craig passed along to him?

I'd handle this and then call Erik to tell him about it as a precaution. "What does your dog look like?"

"She's black and white. About forty-five, fifty pounds."

Heat rushed into my cheeks at the same time as my hands went hypothermia cold. Only one dog here fit that description. If he meant my puppy, then he'd either bought her from the thief or he was the thief.

And I was now all out of benefit of the doubt. "I'm not sure—"

"Why don't I take a look?" He stepped around me, his phone out again. "That'll be the quickest and I'm in a hurry. Lots more shelters to visit if she's not here."

I glanced back over my shoulder and craned my neck. If I could get his license plate number for Erik, he'd be easier to track down.

The front plate holder was empty. Stupid Michigan laws that required only one plate. Who thought that was a good idea anyway?

I hurried after the man. Had I left the office door open, or had I closed it behind me?

He stopped in front of the office. "That's her."

I reached the doorway at the same time as he strode toward my puppy. She growled low in her throat and backed under the desk.

She knew him. And the experience she'd had left her frightened of him. What the heck was I supposed to do now? I could *not* let him take her. I also couldn't let him know I thought he was a criminal. Who knew what he'd do then. Craig's story about giving this guy aggressive dogs to rehabilitate had grown more holes than ancient Swiss cheese.

The man chuckled and knelt down beside the desk. "She likes to play this game at home too."

My lungs felt too sizes too small for my body. "Wait, sir. We have to do release paperwork."

Smart, Nicole. That'd buy you about five minutes.

"But I'm new here, and I'm not sure of exactly what needs to be done. My..." Crap. I couldn't say manager. If he'd been the one to kill Paul and Craig, he'd know there wasn't a manager and that I was making this all up. "A senior employee will be in tomorrow. Would you like me to make an appointment for you to come back and get your puppy then?"

His mouth turned down as the corners. "My fiancée's been crying every night since she disappeared, and I'm the one who forgot to lock the gate, so she's not speaking to me. Can you make an exception?"

Had I not already spoken to the puppy's real owners, and had I not been the daughter of two master manipulators, I would have fallen for it. My heart would have melted at his desperate need to make it right with his fiancée, and I would have broken the rules to help him.

But, for better or for worse, I was my father's daughter and my mother's. When most kids were watching cartoons, I'd been studying cons. This man had listened to what I'd said before about the boyfriend who forgot my coffee and he knew what angle to take.

Now we were locked in a chess game. "I'm really sorry, but I'll lose my job if anyone finds out."

He pressed his hands together like he was praying. "What if I take her home just for tonight and bring her back tomorrow to fill in the paperwork? Then you wouldn't have to get in trouble, and I could make my fiancée happy."

Savvy, making it sound like a win-win compromise. I rolled my lips together. "How about I call someone and ask if that'd be okay? For CYA purposes." I'd actually call Erik and then hope he understood from my disconnected conversation that I needed him.

"No, no. That'd be a ton of hassle for you." He climbed to his feet and swiped at his knees. "I'll tell her that the puppy's safe, and I'll be back to pick the dog up tomorrow."

The smile I gave him felt as fake as if I'd painted it on with clown make-up. "I'll make sure the paperwork is ready for you."

He actually waved at me on his way out.

I watched his car go. My surreptitious attempt to see the back license plate failed as well.

I locked the door and slumped back against the wall. The end to my time "under cover" couldn't come too soon. Most people didn't value their boring lives enough. I'd trade half the money I'd inherited from Uncle Stan for boring right about now.

I headed back for the office and knelt down next to the desk. My puppy still hunched as far as she could get into the corner, tail wrapped between her legs and ears tucked back against her head.

I dialed Erik's number. It went to voice mail. "Give me a call back when you get this. A man came in to the shelter today, and I think he might be involved with Craig and Paul's murders."

None of this made any sense, but my puppy must be part of the key.

I queued up my caller list and stared at Mark's number. Wouldn't it be prudent to brainstorm with someone else? Mark had been my partner in crime-solving last time.

I tossed my phone into the chair. The farther away it was, the less tempted I'd be. I blew out a puff of air. No more thinking about Mark.

I peeked under the desk again. The puppy's tail and ears were no longer crushed to her body, but she showed no signs of coming out. "It's up to you and me. You want to come out and help me?"

Her tail gave two tiny thumps and she laid her head down on her front paws.

"Guess I'm on my own."

I stayed where she could see me and tugged my briefcase over. The papers in Paul's large-dog folder would fall apart if I flipped through them much more, but I couldn't help thinking that they mattered. Paul set them apart rather than cataloguing them like the others.

What if I had it backward? I'd assumed Craig killed Paul because of something despicable on Paul's part related to the large breed or aggressive dogs. Craig's death cast doubt onto that, but I'd still been approaching the case as if Paul's actions were the catalyst.

We didn't know the cause-and-effect sequence. It might have started with Craig, and Paul ended up in the way.

So assuming Erik was right and Paul had been a good guy, why might Paul be paying particular attention to the same type of dogs Craig pretended to euthanize and instead smuggled out of the shelter? It couldn't be that he felt those dogs deserved to die rather than being rehabilitated.

I climbed back to my feet and opened an Internet tab on the computer, then typed *uses for large dogs* into the search bar.

Most of the results that popped up seemed to be products targeted to large dog owners—kennels, durable toys, dosage instructions for medications. The only non-salesy link bore the title *20 Jobs Dogs Have Performed.*

Not exactly focused on large-breed dogs, but most small dogs were used only for companionship, so it was worth a look.

And I had to admit, I couldn't name twenty dog jobs off the top of my head.

I scrolled down the list. Service dogs, therapy dogs, search and rescue, detection of bombs and drugs, guard dogs, racing.

Dogfighting.

A bad taste coated the back of my tongue like I'd bitten into a moldy grape. My parents had accepted almost every client that came to them and was willing to pay, regardless of their guilt or innocence. There'd been only two types of cases they'd turn away—child abuse and animal abuse. My dad used to say kids and animals were the only real innocents in the world.

Craig had been an arrogant jerk, but would he have...?

I sank back to the floor. My puppy's reaction fit with a dog being groomed for fighting. Newly recruited dogs were baited and abused until they turned aggressive. And dogfighting rings were constantly on the hunt for fresh replacements since each fight was to the death. Dogs who already showed aggressive instincts would be ready for the ring faster.

If Paul had suspected what was happening, he might have been investigating. A file folder full of potentially stolen dogs hardly seemed like enough evidence to kill someone over, though. Of course, whatever hard evidence he'd found could have been taken by the killer. It might also be in one of the filing cabinets and the crime scene techs didn't know what they were looking for when they went through the papers.

I glanced at my watch. It was already nearly five o'clock, which meant if I didn't hurry, I'd be cleaning dog runs in the dark. I'd have to check the files after, and if I hadn't heard back from Erik by then, I'd send him a text. I thought about calling the police station directly, but I didn't have anything to report. A man coming to find his lost dog wasn't illegal or even suspicious to most people.

It took close to two hours before I finished, and by then I was hungry and tired, and had no phone call from Erik.

I snagged my belongings and phone and quickly thumb texted *Please call asap. Man came to shelter who might have murdered Paul and Craig.*

Since I only had one free finger, I let the auto-complete do most of the work. Even if I got a word wrong, Erik would get the gist of what I meant.

The puppy was still hiding under the desk. I bent over so I could see her. "Alright, I'm going to grab some human chow. When I get back, you're going to have to come out so we can go home."

I didn't want to scare her by hauling her out from under the desk, but she must be hungry by now. If she was still reluctant when I returned, I'd bribe her with a treat. Once this was settled, we'd need to sign up for some obedience classes. I had zero idea how to train a dog, especially one who'd eventually weigh almost as much as I did.

I closed the office door to keep her from wandering around the shelter while I was gone and shut off all the daytime lights.

The temperature outside seemed to have plunged as soon as the sun went down. In the few feet from the door to my car, my nose and lungs ached. I cranked the heat in the car.

With what self-control I had left, I got myself a chicken Caesar salad with light dressing on the side even though my cravings wanted A Salt & Battery's fried fish and chips.

I took my spare car door clicker from my purse, worked the shelter key off my key ring, and left the car running with everything else inside. Even the five minutes it'd take me to coax the puppy out from under the desk would drop the temperature more than my Southern bones would be happy with. This way we'd be able to return to a toasty car.

I let myself in. The streetlamps outside cast twisted fingers of washed out light along the floor. Shivers crab-walked up my skin. I should have left the lights on.

The quicker I got out of here, the better. We'd go home and I'd turn all the lights on so nothing could hide in the shadows.

I reached for the office doorknob. A beam of light from the kennel area crossed the end of the hall.

My heart slammed into the front of my chest. Someone was back there with a flashlight.

When I'd entered, the front door chime sounded loudly. Whoever it was must have heard me come in.

I edged the office door open, backed in, and inched the door closed again. I ran my hand over the knob, over the side of the door. It didn't lock.

Maybe it was Erik. I'd texted him, after all. Maybe he'd decided to simply come over. The station was only a couple minutes away.

But Erik would have turned on the lights. He wouldn't be poking around in the kennel area with a flashlight.

I shoved my hands into my pockets. No cell phone. I'd thrown it into my purse, and my purse lay on the passenger seat of my car. Why hadn't the town council spent the little extra money to install another phone jack in this closet of an office?

My mind was doing its crazy panic circles thing. Being peeved at the town council wasn't going to save us. I had to focus and figure a way out.

No phone meant I couldn't call 9-1-1. Cement walls and no windows meant the only way out was through the office door.

A warm body pressed against my legs and a tongue touched my palm. I brushed my fingers against the top of the puppy's head. Her whole body trembled, but at least she was out from under the desk.

We'd have to make a run for the front door. I clipped her leash onto her collar.

The whap of footfalls moved slowly down the hall toward us. My breathing echoed in the room like someone played it over a speaker. They'd come looking for me.

Running was no longer an option.

Chapter 17

We had to hide. It was our only chance. Then maybe I could take the intruder by surprise. If I could find a weapon.

The heaviest object in the room was a stapler. Not exactly lethal, but I could probably break a nose with it. The pain might give us a chance to escape.

I dragged the puppy to the left of the door hinges. When the intruder opened the door, we'd be hidden behind it. If we were lucky, he or she would only look inside, think the room was empty, and move on to search the waiting area. Then we could run for the back door. If we weren't lucky, the intruder would come in, and I'd bean him with the stapler.

This seemed like the kind of time when I should pray, but all I could come up with was a pathetic *help!*

The front door chime sounded.

Sweat beaded on my upper lip. Bad. Bad, bad, bad, bad, bad. I had zero chance against two of them. I was going to end up euthanized by pentobarbital like Paul or shot and stuffed in a freezer like Craig. And I hated the cold.

Please, Uncle Stan's God, let them inject me. As much as I hated needles, too, it had to hurt less than if they shot me and missed something vital.

"Police," a voice that sounded like Mark's yelled. "Stop where you are and put your hands up."

A boom from the other side of the door. I stumbled back. Glass shattered somewhere in the front of the shelter, and my ears rang.

It had to be a gunshot. The intruder had a gun, and he'd shot at Mark. Or he'd shot at the person who sounded like Mark.

I couldn't get enough air into my lungs. It felt like someone used my chest as a trampoline.

I had to do something to help. At least I could distract the shooter. I cracked the door and whipped the stapler as hard as I could in the general direction of the shooter.

The shooter swore. A man's voice. His footsteps clunked, fast, back toward the kennel area.

I couldn't hear if the back door gave off its thunk-clank around the cotton stuffed in my ears. It was like trying to listen underwater.

"Nicole!"

It was definitely Mark's voice, but Mark shouldn't be here. He called my name again.

"Here." My legs wobbled underneath me, and I grabbed the edge of the desk. "I'm in here."

The door flew open. I don't know whether he grabbed me first or if I flew to him, but the next thing I knew, he held me tight. I threaded my arms around his waist. His heart pounded under my ear.

"I almost didn't come." Lips pressed into my hair. "If I hadn't come..."

Smart Nicole would have moved away, but I wasn't Smart Nicole right now. Right now I was We-Almost-Died Nicole. And all she wanted was to be held by Mark and to hold him and thank Uncle Stan's God that he was still breathing.

"You have to stop pretending to be the police." My voice sounded frenetic even to me.

"It worked this time, didn't it?" He didn't sound much steadier than I felt.

I nodded my head against his chest. "But he shot at you."

"He missed."

"Semantics." I kept my head tucked down. There was a very good chance that if I looked up, I might kiss him. "What are you doing here?"

"I got your text."

His lips brushed my temple as he spoke, like his head was still bent low over mine, his body a shield between me and whatever danger might still be lurking. A good shiver trailed down my spine.

"You should have called the police," he said.

The cotton was slowly coming out of my ears, but a different fog had invaded my brain, brought on by his closeness. "I couldn't. There's no phone in here, and I left my cell in my car."

Mark broke the embrace. Cold rushed in where his warmth had been.

He pulled his cell phone from his pocket. "Then how did you send me this?"

He swiped his finger across the screen a couple of times, then handed me the phone. The screen cast a sickly yellow-green glow over us.

The screen showed a text from me, sent less than a half hour ago.

Please come asap. Man came to shelter who might have murdered Paul and Craig.

It was my text to Erik, but the phone had filled in *come* for *call* in the first sentence. That I could understand, but how had it gone to Mark?

Oh no.

I barely kept myself from face palming. I'd had Mark's information up on the screen when I'd been tempted to call him earlier. I must have accidentally sent the text to him instead in my rush.

He gave a sharp nod and stepped back, putting more space between us. "It wasn't meant for me, was it?"

Everything in me wanted to lie to him, but I couldn't control my expression fast enough. The truth had to be smeared all over my face.

Sirens wailed and tires screeched in the parking lot.

Mark held out his hand, palm up. I handed back his phone, and he clamped his hand around it.

"Nicole?" This time it was Erik's voice calling for me.

And then all H E double hockey sticks broke loose.

Chapter 18

Mark stormed out the office door. Multiple male voices yelled for him to *stop* and *show us your hands*. Above it all Erik shouted for them to stand down.

I sprinted after him, the puppy bounding at my heels.

Mark stood inches from Erik, fists clenched. He was taller, but Erik had more muscle and enough training to flatten Mark if he actually threw a punch.

I tugged on Mark's sleeve. He'd clearly gone insane. Maybe the bullet nicked his head after all. "Do you have a death wish? They might have shot at you, too, and they wouldn't have missed."

He yanked his arm away. He glared at Erik like he could melt him with Cyclops vision. "What do you think you were doing, putting her in danger like this? Two bodies and you let her work here by herself."

"I didn't let her do anything." Erik's expression made steel look soft. "She's a grown woman and she volunteered."

For a second I considered waving my arms and saying *I'm standing right here.* But it didn't feel like this was simple male chauvinism or Mark's strange jealous streak. It felt like something else was going on. Something with layers and long history and pain.

Quincey Dornbush and the other officer moved down the hall, presumably to clear the building. Their refusal to look at me was a little too studious.

"It's not about her being a grownup," Mark said. "Or a woman. We're supposed to protect the people we love."

His voice broke and he stretched out his fists. Then I saw it on his face, in his eyes. This was about me. And it wasn't.

Erik put a hand on Mark's shoulder. Mark shook it off and strode out the door. His truck tires spit gravel as he peeled out of the parking lot.

My mouth hung open, and I let it. A cold nose shoved my hand. I knelt down and buried my face in the puppy's fur.

Erik's big hand rested on my back and rubbed a soothing circle. "I'm sorry I didn't call you back. I was in a council meeting."

I kept my arms wrapped around my puppy, my chin on the top of her head. "Did Mark call for help?"

"The manager of the shop next door was closing up when the bullet shattered the window. She called 9-1-1."

My mind felt a bit like a chalkboard wiped clean with a dirty brush. I couldn't quite make the words that should be there come into focus.

I stared at the shattered front window. Glass shards splattered the ground inside and out. Triangles of window still hung off the edges of the frame in random spots like broken teeth.

I should be telling Erik about the man who wanted my puppy and about the break-in, which had to be connected. Yet all I could think about was the look on Mark's face. Like something had broken and I'd broken it.

"Mark meant more than this, didn't he?"

Erik's hand stalled, and he cleared this throat. "If he hasn't told you, it's not my place. What I can say is that he blames himself for something that wasn't his fault. You need to ask him for more than that."

I wouldn't be asking him. He seemed to think Erik and I were a couple, and that was for the best. Correcting that misunderstanding had the potential to put me back into the danger zone with Mark. As much as breaking off the friendship now hurt both of us, it'd only hurt more if I'd waited.

Erik reached his hand out to me. I took it and let him help me up.

"Do you feel up to telling me what happened today?"

I nodded. Given all the things I couldn't fix or control, I ought to do something about what I could.

I sat on the floor in Paul's office while my puppy ate and Erik took my statement. The crime scene techs closed off the shelter once again, a large piece of plywood over the blasted out window. This time they also blocked off the street out front in the hope of finding the bullet.

Erik leaned back in the office chair, making it squeak. "Even though I agree with you that the man who was here this afternoon likely came back tonight, we can't prove it."

There lay the problem. Unless the crime scene techs turned up some evidence to tell us who this guy was, we basically had nothing.

"Maybe there'll be a fingerprint. Or a ballistics match to the gun that killed Craig." Assuming they found the bullet that shattered the window.

"Maybe," Erik said. "I still don't see how all of this connects to Paul's death."

If my ideas about what might have happened had been cupcakes, they'd have still been gooey in the middle, but if Erik didn't have any better leads, they might be worth mentioning.

The sooner this case closed, the sooner the shelter could get back to business as usual and the sooner I could take my puppy home and start to build a normal life here in Fair Haven. I didn't know what normal looked like yet, but I'd figure it out. I'd make friends. I'd learn how to cook and how to snowshoe without falling on my face. One day, I'd even stop wishing Mark were part of it.

But I couldn't get to normal until we caught whoever was behind all this chaos.

"I have a theory," I blurted out before I could talk myself out of it. "It might be only slightly less far-fetched than body snatchers and pod people."

Erik smiled. An honest-to-goodness, showing-teeth-and-everything smile.

It was the kind of smile that forced you to smile in return, regardless of what else was going on around you. "Chief Higgins, is that a grin I see?"

The smile grew. "You're something else, Nicole Fitzhenry-Dawes. Has anyone ever told you that before?"

Often, but never in a good way. The old insecurities inside me tried to pounce, but the warmth from his smile drove them back. Why couldn't I have fallen for this man instead? We could have been happy. Emotions were funny, irrational things.

Erik leaned back and crossed his arms over his chest. "So let's hear this theory of yours and then I'll decide whether pod people are a better lead."

"We know Craig was falsifying the paperwork to say he was euthanizing dogs when he was actually giving them to the man I met. I think Paul might have caught on to it and also realized there was an unusually high number of large dogs going missing. From what you've told me, he was the kind of man who would have been worried about the welfare of the animals and might have started investigating himself."

"Do you have a guess about what Paul thought was going on?"

"A dogfighting ring." I closed both eyes as I said it, but then peeked one open to watch Erik's reaction because I couldn't help myself.

Erik rested a hand on top of his head like he'd planned to rub his scalp and forgot. "I'd buy it. After I stepped in to fill Chief Wilson's shoes, I saw how much he'd been covering up in an attempt to look good for his bid for sheriff. But how does the puppy fit into it?"

"I think she was part of Paul's evidence of whatever he found. That's the only thing that makes sense for why the man who came by here would be so desperate to get her back."

Erik's eyebrows lowered like he was mulling over what I'd said.

My defense attorney training was already pointing out all the holes in my theory inside my head. "And I know we technically have nothing right now to directly link her to anything. My guess is that whoever killed Paul took the rest of his evidence."

"Then why not take the puppy at the same time?"

I got up and walked the two steps it took to go back and forth across the office, then went back the other direction. Movement always helped me work through problems.

Nothing came to me. They killed Paul and left the puppy. That was where my theory fell apart.

Chapter 19

Since the police still had the shelter closed down the next day, and since I hadn't had a day off since I got to Fair Haven, I decided I needed a self-care day. I spent the morning in my pajamas, eating the last of the goodies Bonnie sent home with me and reading one of the mystery novels off Uncle Stan's shelves that I hadn't read before.

That's how I planned it, anyway. What it actually turned out looking like was I'd read a couple of pages while standing up, then have to chase down my puppy to find out what object she'd woodchucked. At a particularly interesting part of the book, I lost the heel off one of my shoes, and the banister leading upstairs would need a new coat of varnish to cover up the teeth marks. I swear she thought it was a game called *How much can I destroy before Nicole catches me?*

I made a mental note to find out how long puppies teethed for. My belongings might not survive if it turned out to be more than a week or two. Was this what having children was like?

Bonnie's maple syrup cookies and maple fudge, though, were good enough that I could see selling little gift boxes of them at the pancake house and at the rental shop. If I called up and asked for her recipes, the worst she could say was *no.*

"I'll do better than that," Bonnie said when I posed my request. "I'll teach you how to make them. Half the recipe's in the technique. You're welcome to come over tonight if you're not too tired from work."

That's right. She didn't know I wasn't a full-time shelter employee.

"The shelter's closed today." Which still didn't explain why I didn't need to tend the animals at all today. The break-in wouldn't be public yet, but Craig's murder would have been on the news by now, even if they hadn't released his name. "The shelter's vet tech was murdered."

Bonnie gasped. "I hadn't heard. I'm so glad it wasn't you."

"So am I." Especially given how close I came last night to it being me.

We agreed I'd be at her house in an hour, giving me time to shower and dress and clear anything the puppy could destroy out of the laundry room so I had somewhere to lock her up while I was gone. I'd need to add an extra-large crate to my list of essentials for her.

When Bonnie answered her door, she looked around me as if expecting someone else. "No Mark today?"

Bonnie was nice enough, but I didn't want to discuss my love life—or lack thereof—with her. Given that she'd learned about Paul's murder before it hit the papers, I had a feeling the woman was at the hub of the gossip mill.

"He had to work," I said.

It wasn't a lie. Surely he did need to work today.

Bonnie pinned my arms against my sides and hugged me so tightly in her exuberance that it was going to take the rest of the day for my personal space bubble to bounce back. "Well, I'm glad you could come even if Mark couldn't join in our fun."

She let me go, linked her arm through mine, and led me into the house. I had to kick off my shoes while walking.

"Any sign of Toby?" Bonnie asked.

Based on how long Toby had been missing, I doubted he'd turn up, but I didn't want to take her hope away. "I'm afraid not, but that might change once we have our Facebook page set up. If he lost his collar, someone might have kept him, thinking he was a stray."

"You're right." She patted my arm. "It's just lonely without him. The only family I have left is my nephew out in California, and I only get to see him when he flies me out for Thanksgiving."

She chuckled, but it sounded like a cardboard cut-out of what laughter should be.

Being alone as you aged couldn't be easy. I could see myself ending up in her place thirty or forty years down the road, except I wouldn't even have a nephew to spend Thanksgiving with.

I squeezed her arm closer to my side. "Maybe next time you can give me a cooking lesson at my house. I'll buy all the ingredients. I bet you're as good a cook as you are a baker."

Her face glowed. "I do have some secret family recipes that I think it'd be alright to share with you."

Her smile clogged my throat with a lump I couldn't swallow.

"Now, I'll get the ingredients and bowls and such out if you'll reach down that little green box for me"—Bonnie pointed to the top of her refrigerator—"and find us the recipes. I know 'em by heart, but I want you to be able to see the words on paper. It makes learning easier."

The top of the refrigerator seemed like an odd place to store her recipes, but then everyone had their quirks. Problem was, Bonnie had a few inches of height on me. Even on my tiptoes, I couldn't curl my fingers around the box. "Do you have a stepstool I could use?"

Bonnie turned from the cupboard she'd been facing, her arms piled so high with bowls and pots and measuring cups that her face barely showed over the top. "You could grab a footstool from the living room if you need it."

I dragged it in bum-first because it was too heavy to lift. After I got the recipe box down, I left the footstool next to the fridge in case Bonnie wanted me to put the box back.

I snapped the top open on the recipe box and found the maple syrup cookie recipe near the front. I kept flipping through, looking for the maple fudge recipe as well.

I was almost to the back when I reached a card that didn't have a recipe written on it at all. It listed a website address and what looked like Bonnie's login information. The next cards were the same.

It was smart of her. If anyone wanted to steal her login information, they wouldn't think to look in a recipe box. But finding it made me feel a bit like I was rummaging around in her underwear drawer.

I flipped back to the front to resume my hunt for the maple fudge recipe since I must have missed it the first time through.

My hand stilled on the front card. When the police searched the shelter, they hadn't found anything that looked like evidence Paul had collected or anything to identify my puppy as evidence of wrongdoing. Yesterday Erik and I assumed that meant there was no such evidence and my theory was wrong, but what if Paul hid the evidence because he was afraid someone might come after him? It's what I would do.

I set the cookie recipe on the counter next to Bonnie and handed her the recipe box. "I can't seem to find the fudge recipe. Would you mind? That'll also give me a chance to check in and see when the police might be done with the shelter."

Bonnie bobbed her head and waved me off with a flourish. As I left the room, I could hear her humming a tune.

I called Erik.

"Have you released the scene yet?" I asked when he answered.

"Any time now. And I have some good news. The techs found the bullet lodged in a tree across the street. They'll be able to test it to see if it matches the one we pulled from Craig."

Craig's lifeless face flashed across my mind, and creepy-crawlies skittered over my skin. I'd started seeing a counselor back in DC after my ex's betrayal. It might be wise for me to find one here, too, considering all the things I'd seen.

I licked my dry lips. "Can you hold the scene a little longer?"

"Why?" His voice took on a wary tone. Like he knew I was about to stir up more trouble for him.

"I have a hunch that Paul did find evidence but hid it. I know you can't search his apartment again, so I'm hoping it'll be at the shelter since that's officially a crime scene again."

Erik sighed, but it sounded more like *Okay, I'll bite* than *Why are you wasting my time again?* "Even if that were true, the techs were thorough. If we didn't find his hiding place before, how are we supposed to find it now?"

Bonnie's hiding spot for her passwords was one I'd never have thought of. My best friend Ahanti hid her passport in a plastic baggie on the back of a clock. Hiding spots might be as individual as preferred nail polish colors. Which meant the only one who might know a person's hiding spots would be someone very close to them.

"Melissa might have an idea. If you'd be willing to call her." I used my best *pretty please* voice.

"It might not help."

"I know."

"I'll give it a try."

My cell phone rang as Bonnie and I were finishing up our snack of coffee and fresh maple cookies before tackling the fudge.

Erik skipped the greeting entirely. "You're going to want to see what we found."

I slid a hand over my cell phone. "Would it be alright if we saved the fudge for another day? I'm needed at the shelter."

"Of course!" Bonnie scooped up our plates and slid more cookies into the washed container I'd returned to her. "For when you get hungry," she whispered.

The woman was going to have me in a moo-moo soon if I wasn't careful.

I kept Erik on the phone as I set out in my car. "Where did you find it?"

"Stuffed into the half inch gap under a filing cabinet. Melissa said Paul used to leave messages for her tucked under her filing cabinet when he didn't want anyone else to find them. So I had the team start turning over anything heavy enough that most people wouldn't mess with it."

I almost didn't want to ask the next question. "What was it? That you found."

"A CD."

The thick tone to Erik's voice spoke volumes about how I'd feel when I saw whatever images were on it. A black hole formed in my stomach.

I may have broken a few speed limits on the way to the shelter. Imagining the worst had always been my failing. Once I knew the truth, I could start coping with it.

Erik met me at the shelter door and took me back to the office. He closed the door behind us.

"Take a seat," he said.

It was almost clichéd. I felt like the woman who was asked *Are you sitting down?* before someone gave her life-shattering news.

I sank into the chair anyway.

Erik crouched beside me and slid the mouse away. "I'm only going to show you a short section. You don't need to see it all."

The black hole in the depths of my stomach grew.

He clicked play and the fuzzy still frame on the screen turned into a clearer video. Based on how wobbly the camera shot was, my guess was it'd been taken on a phone. The light was poor, like it'd been shot at night, and at first, the only thing on the screen were the bare, snow-covered branches of a scrubby bush, backlit from light somewhere out of the shot.

Then the angle panned up.

Metal barrels lined the edges of a clearing within the trees. Reflections from the flames carved sharp lines along the snow and cast flares on the phone's screen. A heavy-duty wood and metal snow fence created a ring in the center.

I glanced at Erik. So far the images weren't exactly disturbing or condemning. Something about them even looked vaguely familiar. Probably because I'd been spending so much time out in the sugar bush lately.

I turned my attention back to the screen in time to see the perspective shift again, away from the ring. A navy blue van came into focus. It looked like the same one I'd seen when I caught Craig giving away the aggressive dog.

Cages full of dogs hunched on the ground next to it.

One of them was my puppy. My brain couldn't parse the images I saw next, but I knew now why she'd reacted to the man the way she had. His training methods were brutal.

I looked away.

Erik pressed stop. "Paul kept recording as the spectators arrived and placed their bets and through some of the fights. The recording ends suddenly like he ran out of space or his battery died, but he caught enough to bring charges against a lot of people. My guess is he also stole the Dane puppy either because he couldn't stand to leave her there or he thought she'd serve as additional evidence. We might never know his full reasoning."

Whatever his motivation had been, I was grateful to him for rescuing her rather than leaving her behind. "Great Danes aren't usually used in dogfighting, are they?"

"They're not, but based on what I saw on the rest of the recording, whoever's running this ring is trying to make his fights different." He cringed on the last word.

I didn't envy him or any other police officer the horrible things they had to see on a regular basis. They were heroes for how they shielded citizens, sometimes in ways we didn't even know about.

I pushed the chair back away from the desk until I ran into the filing cabinets just to put space between me and what I'd seen on the screen. "For the sake of the dogs, I was hoping my guess was wrong."

"At least now we know why Paul was killed." Erik ejected the disk from the computer and snapped it back into its case. "I'll have to send this away since we don't have facial recognition software here, but we should eventually be able to identify some of the participants and spectators."

"How long will it take to get some answers?"

Erik pursed his lips. "Depends on how backed up they are, but I'd be surprised if we had names in less than a week or two."

Somehow that felt like a loss rather than a success and that we'd created as many questions as we'd answered. Any of those people could have seen Paul and followed him back here to kill him because they didn't want to be identified, including the man who'd come looking for my puppy. And while the police tried to track them all down, the dogfighting would continue.

A niggling sensation, like a word on the tip of my tongue that wouldn't come, pressed at me. The problem was, I didn't even know what I wanted to describe with the word. All I knew was I couldn't let it rest at this.

"There has to be some way to stop the dogfighting ring now rather than months from now, after more dogs have been tortured and killed."

Erik slid the disk into a brown evidence envelop. "The recording could have been made anywhere. Without more to go on, our best chance is to wait for the facial recognition software to provide us with some hits. I don't like it any more than you do."

The recordings couldn't have been made *anywhere*. They had to be nearby since they were sourcing animals from Fair Haven, both stolen and through Craig. "You said the fights are different. Why? How? Maybe the anomalies will help us narrow the options down."

Erik's forehead crinkled. "I'm not going into how. That's something you don't need to know, and once you did, you'd want to take it back."

He was probably right. I already knew a lot of things I wished I didn't. "Let's stick with *why* then. Why would he make his fights different?"

Erik's look clearly said *how am I supposed to know?*

I curled my fists into balls in my lap to keep from bopping the top of the desk in frustration. It was so petty to miss Mark at a time like this, but he would have spit-balled ideas with me like we had during the investigation of Uncle Stan's murder when we'd visited Beaver's Tail Brewery.

I flattened my palms into my thighs. Maybe that was it. Jason Wood, owner of the brewery, made his awful beers *different* to attract tourists. The organizer of the dogfighting ring might be doing the same. "What do you think?"

"What do I think? I already said I don't know why he'd make his fights different. Seems like the people who want to watch fights wouldn't care whether they were unique or not."

"No, not about that."

"You're not making sense, Nicole. You asked me why they'd make the fights different. I said I didn't know, then you asked me again."

Heat blistered my face. If I wasn't careful, he'd send me home, thinking I was overwrought again. I wasn't. This time I was in complete control. Anger over what these people were doing had burned out all the other emotions. "I guess I forgot to share my idea out loud."

I went over it again, verbally this time.

Erik laid the envelope on the desk and crossed his arms. "I agree with you, but I don't see how that helps us."

His words said *no* but his body language said *yes.* He wasn't packing up any more. He was willing to listen to me at least.

If only I knew where I was going with it. "You said Chief Wilson let things go that he should have stopped, and so on the surface Fair Haven looks like a normal tourist town, but underneath it's catering to people who want darker entertainment on their vacation."

Erik picked up the envelope again and stood. "We're just going in circles."

I slumped in the chair. He was right. I had no idea how to figure this out. "Let's watch the recording again one more time to see if there's anything we missed." I held up a hand before he could protest. "Only what you already showed me. Trust me, I don't want to see any more than that."

He poured the disk out of the envelope. "Only because I hadn't sealed it already. And then you need to leave. I've bent the rules as far as they can go without breaking to let you know this much."

It struck me again what a good man Erik was. If I was a better woman, maybe I'd have fallen for him instead of for a married man I could never have.

Erik started the recording. Same trees. Same clearing. Same barrels. Same ring.

Maybe I was running around trying to catch mosquitos in a jar and wasting Erik's time.

The screen swung to the right again. A smear of blue in the background caught my eye. The screen kept moving before I could get a clear enough look to be sure of what it was, but it felt like I should know. "Scroll it back. Please."

Erik paused the video instead. "I know you want us to solve this tonight, but that's not the way it usually works in investigations. Things take time."

I didn't think we could solve all the pieces of this puzzle tonight, but I might be able to fit another one into place. One that might save a few canine lives. "Trust me. One more time and be ready to pause it when I say so. Then I promise I'll leave if you want me to."

Instead of starting it over, he moused it back bit by bit.

When the blue appeared, I held up my hand. I squinted and leaned closer to the screen.

The pit in my stomach re-opened and swallowed me whole.

The smear of blue was a sap line. The dog fighting ring was holding its events in my sugar bush.

Chapter 20

The military precision snapped back into Erik's bearing. "What do you see?"

Pieces tumbled into place like an avalanche trying to crush me. My lungs didn't want to refill. "They're running it at Sugarwood."

"How do you know?" His voice sounded official again, more like a police officer and less like a tolerant friend.

I pointed out the blue line on the screen. My finger shook. "I've been walking those sap lines, checking for damage. I'd recognize them in my sleep."

Oh no. The packed down circles I found. Those must be...

I covered my face with my hands. I took a picture to show to Russ, and then I'd forgotten all about it. My inexperience with what was normal and abnormal in nature had cost so much time, and I made it worse by getting distracted.

I sucked in a breath and lowered my hands. Erik was watching me as if he wasn't sure whether to comfort me or push me for more information.

I flicked through my phone until I found the picture and turned it toward him. "I found two separate rings in the snow like this one. When I first told Russ about it, he thought it was probably from a wolf that'd caught something. I took this picture to show him because it seemed too big. Does that look like it could have been made by the same setup as in Paul's video?"

Erik was already tapping at my phone. "I'm emailing these to myself."

I groaned. I should have put it together sooner. "And that's why a man who hated the cold was renting snowshoes. He must have followed the van until they headed into the bush, where he'd have been easily spotted if he kept after them. So he started renting snow shoes to figure out where, exactly, they were holding the fights."

"Paul rented snowshoes from Sugarwood?"

I nodded.

He handed my phone back. "I need you to show me where you found these spots. After what happened here tonight, I doubt they'll be hosting a fight this evening. Once I see the location, we can work on setting up surveillance so there'll be no way they continue to get away with it."

***

Within a half hour, we were at Sugarwood, I'd texted Russ to have him feed and walk my puppy, and I'd grabbed two sets of snowshoes and gear from the rental shop.

"I bet there's a good story behind this." Dave handed me the snowmobile keys. "No one goes out right before dark without a good story."

I swear he was almost drooling over the idea of new fodder for his novel. "I'll tell you all about it later, okay?"

He settled back at the desk, his pen and notebook already out again. "Sure. Oh, wait." He looked up. "You want me to keep the shop open for you? Rentals are all supposed to be back by five because we don't allow non-employees on the grounds after dark, so I'm usually gone by 5:30."

I waved at him on my way out the door. "No need to wait up. I'll keep them at my place until tomorrow morning."

He didn't reply. When I glanced back, his head was already bowed over his notebook, his tongue peeking out between his lips.

I dragged everything out the door to where Erik waited by the snowmobile. He helped me secure our gear to the trailer.

He motioned to the snowmobile. "I'd say ladies first, but it's really more about you being the driver in this case."

I swung over the seat and Erik slid on behind me. He wrapped his hands around my waist. I expected to feel some zing of energy, but nothing happened. It was sort of like hugging Russ.

I was clearly a lost case.

The snowmobile roared to life and I angled us down the trail I used to get close to my section of the bush.

We were still a minute or two from where I'd planned to stop when Erik squeezed my waist.

He brought his head down as close as he could around our helmets. "Stop here," he yelled.

I braked, and as soon as we slid to a stop, he leaned around me and turned the snowmobile off.

I shifted sideways. "What's going on?"

He pointed to the right and I followed with my gaze. At first I thought he might have imagined something in his desire to find the spot.

Then I saw it. The faint flicker of fire light.

We were supposed to simply identify the likeliest spots for the dog fighting ring to setup, and instead they were in the middle of setting up for a fight.

I swung my leg over the snowmobile and sat sideways on it like a bench. "What do we do now?"

He hopped off the machine and strapped his snowshoes onto his boots. "We make sure those lights are on your property and then we call it in."

I joined him and worked the pair of snowshoes I'd brought for myself onto my feet. I'd forgotten to grab boots, and my running shoes didn't fit correctly. The snowshoes flopped like droopy dog ears every time I lifted my foot. But they'd do in a pinch. "Don't we need proof of wrongdoing?"

"Not if they're on your property after you close to the public."

So, as long as we waited for five o'clock, I could call them in for trespassing. That was smart. We wouldn't have to wait for evidence of something illegal, and we wouldn't have to get close enough that I could identify the man who'd come to the shelter or close enough to be sure of what was happening. Getting that close would put us at risk of being spotted.

I fought my way through the snow behind Erik, allowing him to break the trail. Puffs of white, almost like smoke, billowed up from his face as his breath hit the cold air. I'd need a long soak in a very hot tub after this to take the chill out of my body. Even the exertion of trekking through the snow in Uncle Stan's oversized coat wasn't keeping me warm enough.

As we drew closer, Erik stopped behind a wide maple and motioned for me to join him. "Can you see if they're on your property?"

I peered around the tree. We were close enough now that I could see figures silhouetted against the flames. Based on how few of them there were, the fights hadn't begun yet. Thank God.

"Nicole?" Erik's voice had an urgent edge to it.

I squinted into the growing darkness. They were close to the right edge of the property. Russ might have been able to wager an accurate guess from this distance whether they were technically on Sugarwood grounds or not, but I wasn't familiar enough with the landmarks. "I can't tell. We'll have to get closer."

Erik's arms twitched like he wanted to cross them over his chest but couldn't because of the snow shoe poles. "I'm not taking you any closer. What do I need to look for?"

His body had a coiled look to it, like he was tense and ready to react without being stiff. It must be what he'd looked like in combat.

My core went as cold as my skin. The reading I'd done online about dogfighting rings said they also usually had connections to illegal drugs and weapons. Considering they'd already killed two people, it's not like they'd hesitate to add a couple more to the list, even a police officer. Erik had his service weapon, but if they spotted us, we'd still be outnumbered.

It'd be stupid to argue with the man with the training at a time like this. "The boundaries are marked by small yellow stakes. I don't remember how far apart they're placed exactly. You might have to look around a bit."

He unbuttoned the heavy outer jacket he'd added from the rental shop and dropped it to the ground. I was about to ask him what he was doing when he checked his weapon. He wanted to be sure he had easy access to it.

I tried to swallow, but my larynx seemed to be completely frozen. "What do you want me to do?"

"Stay out of sight for now. If you hear anything that makes you think they saw me, you get back to the snowmobile, call for help, and leave."

It felt cowardly to abandon him if something went wrong, but he wouldn't have brought me in the first place if we suspected they'd be running another round of fights tonight, so close to the break-in at the shelter.

There was one major problem with his plan, though. "Cell service is patchier out here than in the rest of Fair Haven."

Erik cursed and fished his cell phone from his pocket. He unzipped his lighter jacket and used the sides as a light shield, then woke the phone. He cursed again.

He didn't have signal.

"Russ let you come out here without any way to call for help?"

One part of me wanted to respond with a snarky flare-up and tell him he was sounding like Mark now. I bit that response back. "Of course not. We use walkie-talkies." I patted the spot where the utility belt hung around my hips, underneath Uncle Stan's oversized dress coat. I might not have remembered to bring the belt and walkie-talkie on my own, but I'd left it on the sled the last time I went out. Erik didn't need to know that, though. "But it depends on someone listening in one of the buildings. We only have people monitoring the channel if they know someone's out here."

Erik ran a gloved hand over the top of his head. "Try the walkie-talkie then, but you go one way or another. Promise me."

I clutched my snowshoe poles so tightly my knuckles ached. "I promise."

He moved off, perpendicular to the firelight at first. The farther away he got, the more aware of the darkness I became. Sometime after we left the snowmobile, the last rays of sunlight died and the moon hadn't risen over the treetops yet.

The shivers that ran over my body were only half due to the cold. I leaned my head back against the tree, wrapped my scarf over my mouth and nose for warmth, and hugged my arms around my body.

There isn't anything in the dark that isn't there in the light. There isn't anything in the dark that isn't there in the light.

Of course, in the light, I could see it and prepare for it. And things came out at night that wouldn't be moving around in the daylight.

"Stop it," I whispered to myself.

I closed my eyes. At least then I could pretend the darkness came from my eyelids.

With my eyes closed, the sounds that already carried on the night air amplified. The occasional snap of wood in the fires. Voices, but the words weren't clear enough for me to hear. The screech of an owl hunting.

I focused on the breeze through the trees, and my heart rate came back to normal. I reopened my eyes.

A gunshot shattered the stillness.

Chapter 21

I crouched and threw my arms over my head. It wouldn't have protected me from a bullet, but my body reacted before I could think.

Erik's instructions to run warred with my instincts to hide or run in his direction rather than away from it. The more logical part of me knew that running directly into danger wouldn't help him as much as going for help, the way he'd ordered me and the way I promised.

I plunged out from behind the tree as fast as my snowshoes would allow. The ring of light was in chaos now. Yelling, and another shot rang out.

A bellow that sounded like "There's another one!" came from behind me.

I glanced back over my shoulder. Two shadowy figures had broken off from the lighted area and were heading in my direction. It was clear from the smoothness of their movements that they were more skilled on their snowshoes than I was.

My lead might not last long enough to reach—

I went down face first into the snow.

I rolled onto my back, reaching for the ties on my snowshoes. I yanked them both off, scrambled to my feet, and plowed forward.

I sank into the snow deep enough that it was like trying to run through water, but it was still better than with the ill-fitting snowshoes on. The men behind me had already gained ground. Another fall like the first one and they'd be on top of me.

Uncle Stan's heavy coat now dragged behind me, along the tops of some of the bigger snow drifts, slowing me down further. I shucked it off. Frostbite wouldn't matter if I was dead, and I was certain now that I'd be dead if they caught me.

A shot splintered the bark on of the trees to my left. For a second I wanted to scream at them for hurting one of my trees, and then common sense kicked in— they'd been aiming for me, not the tree.

I dodged to the right, off the path Erik and I had started to beat down on our way there. It'd be slower going for me, but slower going for them as well, and they wouldn't have quite as clear a shot at me. My best chance to survive seemed to be to weave and dodge.

The sugar bush was too well-tended to have much underbrush, which left me no way to hide unless they lost sight of me.

They might in the dark, if I could put space between us.

I picked up my pace. My lungs and thighs burned—one from cold, the other from exertion—and sweat dampened the collar of my shirt. I grabbed a branch and used it to help swing me around at another right angle. My lack of snowshoes at least gave me that advantage.

Off to the left, a spiky blob loomed in the darkness. One of the piles of cleared underbrush Russ had told me about? When Uncle Stan died suddenly last fall, they'd run out of time to finish hauling away all the clean-up piles.

I took another sharp turn, gathered up the last of my flagging energy, and sprinted forward. I dove behind the brush pile and into a little hollow in the pile, pulled as many loose pieces as I could down around me for cover, and curled myself into a ball.

My breathing was still too loud and ragged. I balled my scarf over my face and forced myself to breath more slowly.

Please let them pass me by. The mantra turned into a prayer somewhere around the third or fourth repetition. *Please let Erik still be alive.*

The crunch and squeak of the men's snowshoes drew alongside the brush pile.

"Check behind," one of them said.

I couldn't see out well enough to know exactly where he was, but the footfalls moved closer.

"Not back here," a deeper voice said.

Their discussion of whether to keep searching for me or head back faded away.

I let out a breath. Chills wracked my body and my teeth chattered. I hadn't noticed the cold while I was running, but now my damp clothes allowed it to soak into my skin, into the blood in my veins.

I had to get back to the snowmobile and go for help for my sake now as well as Erik's. If I stayed out here much longer, I'd catch hypothermia.

I crawled out from my hole. The bush felt abnormally quiet now and the dark pressed down on me again, threatening to bow my legs. Either that or they were weakened from the cold.

I trudged back in the direction I'd come and stopped. I pivoted slowly in a circle. All the trees looked the same. And with so many people traipsing through the bush, checking lines, adventuring on rented skis and snowshoes, and, apparently, attending dogfights, I couldn't tell the path I'd made from all the others.

I'd changed directions so many times in my mad dash that I didn't know where I was.

Worse, I didn't know where the snowmobile was.

Chapter 22

I was going to die out here. In the fracking Michigan cold. Any other way of dying would be better. I'd much rather drown for instance. Or fall from a ledge and break my neck.

"Pull it together, Nikki. You're rambling again."

I patted my cheek in lieu of slapping some sense into myself the way they had in an episode of *Myth Busters* I watched one night when I couldn't sleep.

"Think it through. There has to be a way out."

It'd felt slightly warmer curled up in the brush pile. I'd climb back in. It wouldn't keep me alive if I ended up stranded out here for the rest of the night, but it might buy me a few extra minutes. I'd cling to every minute I could beg, borrow, or steal.

I worked my way back into my brush pile hole and tugged out the walkie-talkie. I pressed the button. "Is anyone at Sugarwood receiving this?"

I let the button go. No one responded. But I'd forgotten to say *over* again. Maybe the person on the other end didn't know I was done, the way Russ hadn't.

"Is anyone at Sugarwood receiving this? Over."

The line lay silent, and my watch read 5:41. Now that the rental shop was closed for the night, Dave would be gone and not monitoring the radio. Noah and Russ should both be in their homes already, and neither of them probably listened to the walkie-talkie receiver for the fun of it at night.

I smacked a hand into a branch beside me. So my choices were to stay here and keep trying in vain to raise someone on the walkie-talkie...and likely freeze to death. Or I could go out searching for the snowmobile...and likely freeze to death.

Or I could try to walk back to the Sugarwood buildings. If I knew which direction to head in, that option gave me the best chance of success for both surviving and getting help for Erik, assuming he was still alive. If I went in the wrong direction, I'd still end up dead from hypothermia.

I'd rather die trying than die curled up in a giant pile of sticks.

I re-holstered the walkie-talkie, crawled out of the hole, and wound my scarf over my head so that it covered as much of my face as possible. If I made it out of this alive, I'd like to also keep my nose. It was one of my best features.

The question now became which direction to head. I turned slowly in a circle. Everything looked the same in all four directions, just trees and the occasional blue sap line.

Sap lines!

Next time I saw Russ, I was going to plant a big kiss on his wrinkly cheek. I could follow the sap lines back to the sugar shack.

I slogged through the snow to the nearest one and trailed along beside it.

Time seemed to flatten after that, and I refused to check for fear knowing how long I'd been out here—and how our chances of survival dropped the longer I was—would make me give up. All I could focus on was dragging one foot in front of the other.

With each step, the snow seemed thicker and deeper, even though I knew logically that couldn't be possible.

I tripped, grabbed for something to stabilize me, missed, and tumbled to my knees.

It was important I get up. That little voice inside my head that always sounded suspiciously like my mother yelled at me to get up. But my legs seemed to be made out of soft-serve ice cream.

I'd failed. I wasn't going to make it after all, which also meant help wasn't coming for Erik. I'd failed us both.

My throat clogged and I swallowed hard. For once my parents were right. Crying wouldn't help. The tears would only freeze on my cheeks.

And as long as I was conscious, I had to try something.

I fumbled with the holder for the walkie-talkie, my fingers about as limber as German sausages. As futile a hope as it was, Russ or Noah might have forgotten to turn off one of the receivers and might have gone back to one of the buildings for something. It was the epitome of the old grasping-for-straws cliché, but I had to grasp something.

"Sugarwood. Need help." My words came out all slurry and garbled. Even if I reached someone, they'd have fun trying to understand me now. "Over."

"Nicole?" Dave's voice crackled through the walkie-talkie. "Is that you?"

I stared at the handset, blinking around frost-crusted eyelashes. Dave shouldn't still be in the rental shop at this time of night. Did hypothermia cause auditory hallucinations?

I struggled to pull the frayed ends of my thoughts back together. "Are you at Sugarwood? Over."

His laughter came through the handset first. "Yeah. After you left, the ideas started flowing."

"I'm stranded in the bush." Each word took me forever to form. "Need help."

"I thought I'd just write a couple of pages after locking up, before I went home, so I didn't lose the ideas. Guess I lost track of time instead."

He kept rambling like he didn't hear me.

Grrr. He didn't hear me. Russ said these things didn't work like cell phones. Until he let go of the button on his end, he wouldn't hear anything I said.

"Over," he finally said.

I was struggling to keep my eyes open now. That couldn't be a good sign. "I. Need. Help."

"Are you drunk? I can barely understand you." He chuckled. "I've heard of drunk dialing before, but never drunk radioing. Wonder if I can fit that in my story somewhere..."

Dear Lord, let him have released the button. "Stranded in bush. No coat."

"What?" His voice lost the *I'm only half listening to you* tone it'd had before. "Are you serious? Hang on. I'm calling Russ."

"Hurry," I croaked.

"I have him now and we're getting out some maps, but you're going to have to tell us where you think you are. The bush is too big otherwise."

I forced my brain to focus. "Started near where I was checking sap lines." My teeth chattered hard enough to send spikes of pain down into my jaw. "Hid in a brush pile, then followed the lines toward Sugarwood."

The pause after I finished felt like years.

"Okay," Dave finally said. "Russ is taking the other snowmobile and he called Noah. He'll start looking for you with the sleigh too. And I've called 9-1-1. Hang on, okay? Stay awake."

Easy for him to say. Course anything was easier for him to say. My body felt like I'd overdosed on sleeping pills.

"Nicole! You need to answer me."

I could hear the frantic note in his voice now, but responding to it took energy I didn't have.

I didn't remember closing my eyes, but the next thing I knew, Dave's face peered into mine and he called my name.

My eyes must have drifted shut again, because when I opened them the next time, the forest around me was moving.

I blinked and my vision cleared. The forest, it turned out, was standing still, and I was moving. Trees and the dark sky splattered with stars slid slowly past above me.

I tried to move my arm, but a blanket pinned it next to my body. Whatever I laid on was hard and straight. And I was warmer.

This was definitely *not* how I pictured heaven. "I'm not dead."

The words came much easier, and they sounded the same when they came off my lips as they had in my head.

"Nope. You're still alive." Dave's voice floated down to me from somewhere above and behind my head. "I wasn't sure when I found you though. I radioed Russ and Noah to let them know. We're just about back now anyway."

I'd been thawing for a while then. "How did you find me?"

"Russ and Noah were gonna start at the back of the bush and work forward, but when you stopped talking to me, I figured I oughtta start from the front just in case you got farther than we thought. So I packed up a sled and snowshoed out. It's a good thing you didn't have your coat on after all, too. That green color in your sweater isn't found in nature."

"They call it evergreen."

Dave snorted.

I freed my arms and peeled down the blanket. Turned out Dave had layered me in two blankets, not just one. Little bubbles of warmth shifted with me as I moved. I plucked one out. He'd packed me in with a whole crate full of the snap-and-go glove warmers. Smart man.

I squiggled around until I could sit up a little while keeping the bottom blanket wrapped around me. I was safe, but Erik wasn't yet. "I need to call the police."

Dave pointed ahead of us. I craned my neck so I could see what he was pointing at. Red, blue, and white lights flashed through the trees.

"You can talk to them live as soon as we pass this last row of trees."

Chapter 23

"He's awake and asking for you."

For a second I didn't recognize the disembodied voice coming from my cell phone or what they were talking about. Then it clicked.

I rubbed a hand over my eyes. "Thanks, Officer Dornbush. We'll be right up. What room is he in?"

Quincey Dornbush gave me the number.

I slid my feet to the floor. The row of plastic hospital chairs I'd been sleeping on had left a matching line of aches down my side. Russ sat next to me, his head propped against the wall, his mouth hanging open. A soft snore vibrated his chest.

Officer Dornbush had said I should go home and sleep, but since Russ had already put my puppy to bed, I wanted to stick close so I'd be around when Erik came out of surgery. The search-and-rescue team had found him shot through the shoulder out in the woods. Apparently, the cold had worked in his favor. The doctor thought that if he'd been warmer, he'd have been dead by the time they found him.

And since I stayed at the hospital, Russ, of course, insisted on staying with me, just like Uncle Stan would have.

I gently shook him. He jerked awake with a snort-cough, and we headed upstairs.

We found Officer Dornbush in the chair next to Erik's bed. As we entered, he stopped mid-sentence and jumped to his feet. He motioned me to the chair.

Erik's face had the same gray cast as edible kindergarten paste. An IV still poked from the back of his hand, and his left shoulder was in a sling. He smiled up at me, then winced.

I dropped into the chair. "Next time," I said, "I vote we take backup even if we don't expect the bad guys to be there."

His eyebrows drew down. "Next time?"

I'd forgotten that joking wasn't really his thing. I held up my hands. "Kidding. How do you feel?"

"About like I look, I imagine."

I almost said *That bad, huh?* but thought better of it. He might not interpret that as teasing, either.

Erik jerked his chin toward Officer Dornbush. "I asked Quincey to bring you up so you could hear the news as well."

If it'd been Mark, I would have wilted because he hadn't called me up, desperate to know that I was okay. With Erik, though, it seemed natural that he called me up to share about the case. Our relationship was a different one—more like an indulgent older brother-type with his kookie little sister—but it felt right. I was starting to like it rather than regret it.

I looked up at Officer Dornbush.

He folded his hands in front of him. A smile split his face. "Well, you'll be happy to know that we caught the organizer of the dogfighting ring. His name is Al Cahoon. The gun he had on him matches the bullet we pulled from our second victim and the one we found in the tree after your intruder shot at Mark. Once we have a chance to test it, we're confident it'll match the one the doctor took from Chief Higgins' shoulder as well. He lawyered up, but with all the guns and drugs we found, along with the dogs, his lawyer advised him to take the plea. He confessed to all three."

I grinned at Erik.

I wasn't sure whether it was the wound and blood loss or something else, but his face looked drawn. "And Paul's murder?"

Officer Dornbush widened his stance a touch as if bracing himself. "Unfortunately not."

I felt my head shaking, but it was almost as if it belonged to someone else. "He's obviously lying."

Officer Dornbush and Erik exchanged a look. I glanced at Russ, but he shrugged. He seemed to be on my side with thinking Cahoon must be the killer.

Erik fisted his good hand on top of his blanket. "He's never getting out, Nicole. Another murder charge wouldn't lengthen his sentence. What he bargained for was the ability to choose where he'd spend the rest of his life."

"Sometimes," Officer Dornbush said, "crimes go unsolved. This might end up being one of them."

It didn't make sense. He had to be lying. We'd done all this to find Paul's murderer. To come up empty-handed now was unbearable.

But the part of me that would always be governed by my upbringing and my training as a lawyer knew the truth. The hole in my theory was still there. If they'd killed Paul, why not take my puppy at the same time? Even if they couldn't find the disk Paul hid under the filing cabinet, my puppy was in the kennel, in clear sight.

"What reason did Cahoon give for killing Craig?" I asked.

Officer Dornbush's at-attention stance relaxed like he was happy I'd moved away from asking about Paul. "Cahoon knew someone stole the Great Dane he was training up, and he figured—rightly—that whoever took her wanted to expose his business. Her microchip would have made her original owner easy to track and her theft easier to prove. So he had his contacts looking for the dog. Craig must have figured out she was at the Fair Haven shelter because he told Cahoon he had her."

It was no wonder my instincts had been going as haywire as a compass around a magnet. I wanted to like Craig because he worked at the shelter and said he was helping aggressive dogs, but subtle cues must have been triggering my subconscious not to trust him.

My legs jittered with the need to move. I rose to my feet.

Russ frowned and poked a stiff finger toward the chair. Since I'd warmed up and eaten, I felt much better, but Russ continued to act like I'd come down with pneumonia and needed to rest.

I glared at him, but dropped back into my seat. Arguing with him now about my well-being would only sidetrack us from what I really wanted to talk about.

When I looked back at Officer Dornbush, his grin was much too amused. I narrowed my eyes at him as well, and he ran a hand over his mouth. It softened the grin but didn't wipe it away completely.

I slid my hands back and forth along the arms of the chair since I wasn't allowed to pace the room. "Why would Cahoon kill him if Craig was going to give him my Great Dane puppy?"

"The dog wasn't there when Cahoon came to pick her up. Craig swore he didn't know where she went, and Cahoon didn't believe him. He assumed Craig was going to use the dog to blackmail him for a higher cut instead. Apparently, he got a piece of the profits from any dog he turned over to Cahoon's operation."

My stomach turned over, and I was suddenly glad Russ made me stay seated. "It's my fault. I took the puppy home with me."

"It's not your fault," three male voices said at once.

It was so sitcom-ish that I wanted to crack up, but I held my laughter inside. If I started to laugh, the rest of my self-control might go with it and hysterical laughter could end up in tears. "At least I know you're all in agreement."

I leaned back in my chair and a yawn broke free. The sleep I'd gotten on the hospital waiting room chairs hadn't made up for all the energy I'd burned trekking through the woods. It was time for us to leave soon since Erik couldn't be feeling any perkier than I was. "What'll happen to the dogs?"

Erik shifted his position on the bed like he couldn't find a comfortable spot to rest. "We'll return the stolen dogs to their owners, and the others will be sent out of state for rehabilitation and adoption."

This time my yawn broke free. "Why out of state?"

Erik cleared his throat, and I sat up straight. His nervous tic didn't bode well for what was coming next.

"Maybe we should talk about it when you've had a chance to rest up," he said.

It felt like someone had surgically implanted a plank into my spine. Even my mother couldn't have critiqued my posture. "I'd rather know now."

"Michigan law prohibits dogs confiscated from a dogfighting ring from being adopted within the state."

The pause stretched as if he was hoping I wouldn't make him spell it out. I knew what he meant, but I was going to make him say it anyway. Because I didn't know if it would sink in as reality unless I heard it out loud.

His jaw was tight, like he didn't want to say it any more than I wanted to hear it. "I'm sorry, Nicole, but that includes the Great Dane puppy."

Chapter 24

A worker from the Michigan Humane Society was at my door precisely at nine o'clock the next morning. Any other time I'd waited for someone to deliver or fix something, they'd been late or had told me they couldn't specify a time. The one instance when I'd wanted extra time, the woman had to be prompt.

I left the puppy's little purple collar on her, attached the matching leash, and sent along the toy she seemed to have selected as her favorite. From my time fake working at the shelter, I knew the dogs there didn't have toys, and a puppy should have a toy at least. At the last second, I threw all the other toys I'd bought for her into a plastic bag and handed them over as well.

Moping after she was gone might not have been the most mature response, but I moped around the house for the rest of the morning. By early afternoon, I couldn't stand the emptiness anymore. I needed to do something valuable.

I called Russ, but he refused to allow me to work.

I walked another lap around the house. My puppy's crate stared at me as I passed.

Sometime today they'd probably be releasing the stolen dogs back to their owners. If I could find out when that was happening and who was handling it, I might be able to wheedle my way in and go along. Those were visits I'd love to be a part of, especially since I'd met some of the owners through our lost pets group. And there was one dog especially that I'd like to know if they found and would be returning to his own-er—Bonnie's Toby.

I called the police station. When the receptionist answered the phone, I asked for Officer Dornbush.

"He's not at the station right now," the man said. "You can leave a message if you'd like."

Drat. If I couldn't reach someone today, they might have returned all the dogs or at least have made arrangements for who would do it before I could take part. "Could you just tell him that Nicole Fitzhenry-Dawes called? He knows my number." As hard as I tried to hide it, a note of disappointment filtered into my voice.

"Dawes? Like Stan Dawes?"

I swear sometimes it seemed like my uncle had been the town celebrity. "My uncle."

"Aw, man. He was a stand-up guy. Hang on and let me radio Quincey. If he's okay with it, I'll give you his cell phone number."

Thank you, Uncle Stan. I might have a chance to be part of something good after all.

The man was back in under a minute. "You got a pen?"

I jotted down Quincey's number.

"I thought you'd be resting up," he said when I called him.

He clearly didn't know me very well. "I did that this morning."

He chuckled. "How can I help you, Nicole?"

"It's actually how I can help you." Even if they didn't approve of my life choices, my parents would surely have approved of my ability to put a spin on things to get my way. And, after all, it was for a good cause. "I thought you might be in need of an extra set of hands when it comes to returning the stolen dogs."

"That won't be until the end of the week since the dogs still need to be cleared by a vet. What we really need is someone to go through the pictures of the re-covered dogs and help figure out which ones might be stolen."

I hadn't thought about that, but it wasn't like the dogs could raise a paw and declare that they had an owner other than Cahoon. I apparently skipped over more than one step in the process. "The Lost Pets group I'm part of would be happy to do that. We have the pictures of all the dogs that were reported missing."

"I'll clear it with Erik, but I should be able to have the photos over to you later this afternoon."

I jigged a happy dance around my kitchen. I might have lost my puppy, but I could still help other people get theirs back.

As soon as I hung up with Officer Dornbush, I called Bonnie. "Get the group together. I have great news."

The next evening Bonnie met me at her front door, dislocated a couple of my ribs with her hug, and dragged me down the hall.

"Everyone's here," she said.

She released my hand and sailed into the living room. Her excitement loosened the knot that'd been wrapped around my heart since the Humane Society took my puppy. Last night, after the euphoria of being able to help return dogs to their owners wore off, and I found myself in my dogless bed, I'd cried myself to sleep.

I kicked my shoes back down the hall toward the front door and continued on into the living room after her.

I stuttered to a stop one step into the room and my heart felt like it tumbled out of my chest and hit the floor.

Mark sat on the same side of the love seat as he had when we came to the first meeting together. This time, though, he sat as far toward the arm as the sofa would allow. And he didn't look at me, like we were back in high school pretending not the notice the person we secretly had a crush on.

The others in the room were all looking at me and smiling or calling out greetings. I couldn't keep hovering here in the doorway.

The only remaining seat was next to him unless I wanted to stand or sit on the floor. And I was *not* sitting next to Mark on that love seat since last time it'd been determined to dump me into his lap.

I moved over to the coffee table in the middle and poured the photos out. You'd think I'd poured out candy with the feeding frenzy of grasping hands. Part of it was probably a desire to see if their own missing dog was among them. "There are a lot of them, so I hope you all brought the files from last time. We can all start picking out the ones that look like they might match and comparing them."

"I was telling my husband that I can't believe this was happening here in Fair Haven," the young mom—I think her name was Dana—said. She rocked the car seat holding her baby with one foot while sifting through a handful of photos. She reminded me a bit of an octopus with her multi-tasking. "But I feel like getting some of these dogs back to their owners is just the start of great things. It'll help raise awareness for what we're trying to do."

I crouched down and reached for a few of the remaining photos on the table at the same time as Mark did. Our fingers bumped, and a tingle shot up my arm like I'd touched an exposed wire instead. We both jerked our hands back.

My gaze snagged on his. I wanted to say *I'm sorry*. I wanted to say *It's not you, it's me*. I wanted to say so many things, but there couldn't have been a worse time to say any of them even if they wouldn't have sounded clichéd.

"It's Toby!" Bonnie screeched.

I lost my balance and toppled backward, landing soundly on my backside and feeling as graceful as an upended crab. From now on, no squatting for me. I could either stand or sit. I was tired of tumbling over and bashing my butt.

Bonnie had turned the picture around and was showing it to everyone. "I knew it. I said the reason we weren't finding our dogs was Paul. I knew he had to go if we wanted to get them back. Everything's been better since Nicole took over."

Dana and the elderly man sitting next to Mark were suddenly talking over each other, agreeing with her about how the shelter would be in much better hands, but all I could hear was the way she'd phrased it.

I knew he had to go...

She'd said something very similar the first time I met her.

Numbness spread through my limbs. It couldn't be. Bonnie was sweet and gentle. She baked fudge and cookies and put bowties on her dog. She wasn't a killer.

Everyone is capable of murder, my dad's voice said in my head. *The only difference is in what it takes to push them to it.*

"Nikki?" Mark's voice cut through my haze. "Are you okay?"

The tsunami of attention shifted in my direction.

Bonnie hovered over me and her hands fluttered around me, the picture of Toby still flapping along with them. "Geez-o-pete, she's pale. What's wrong?"

I couldn't tell them the truth. It might not even be the truth. And I couldn't think here on the floor with all of them staring at me and talking at once.

I lifted my arm. "I think I might have twisted my wrist when I fell."

Mark knelt down beside me. I guess an injury trumped his desire to pretend like I didn't exist. "I'll take her to the kitchen for some ice and have a look."

Bonnie patted him on the shoulder. "Oh, that's a good idea. We'll let the doctor handle it."

Mark gave a wry smile that barely made him dimples peek out. "Live people aren't exactly my specialty, but I think I can handle a sprained wrist."

He helped me to my feet, the warmth of his hand eating through my clothes to my skin like acid and fogging my brain even further.

Bonnie's kitchen and living room were separated by one of those old-fashioned doors that swung both ways. We pushed our way through and the door whapped back and forth in progressively tinier movements until it finally stopped.

Mark reached for my wrist, and I stepped back. I couldn't think straight with him touching me, and I needed to think clearly because my suspicion was horrible. Almost as bad as when I'd suspected Russ of killing Uncle Stan.

Mark's expression darkened.

Crap. He'd completely misinterpreted my actions.

He shoved his hand toward me, palm up. "Look, I know that—"

"It's not what you think." The words eerily echoed the ones I'd said to Erik about him not that long ago. I flopped my wrist around. "I'm not hurt."

Mark cocked an eyebrow. "Okay. You want to tell me what we're doing back here, then?" A ghost of his old smile slipped out, complete with heartbreaking dimples. "Surely it's not because you were desperate to be alone with me."

A little bubble of hope rose up in me that maybe we could find a way to coexist in Fair Haven and be cordial when we encountered each other even if a friendship was out of the question.

Bonnie's loud laugh carried from the other room, and the bubble deflated.

If I was right, I was about to lose yet another friend.

Chapter 25

I lowered my voice. "I think Bonnie might have killed Paul."

The expression on his face was what I would have expected if I'd made a lewd joke. "That's not funny."

"It wasn't meant to be."

"I thought the organizer of the dogfighting ring killed Paul."

I filled him in on what I'd learned the night before.

Mark sat heavily on one of Bonnie's kitchen table chairs. "You could be wrong. We were wrong about Russ."

We had been wrong about Russ. But I didn't think that was the case this time. All the clues I should have seen were falling into place in my mind like a row of dominoes that'd been tapped on one end.

"When she came to the animal shelter my first day there, Paul's death hadn't been announced publicly yet, but she still knew about it."

"That doesn't mean she killed him. News in this town spreads faster through the gossip mill than it ever has through real news channels."

True enough. This time, though, Erik had been carefully trying to keep it quiet for as long as possible because he hadn't wanted to deal with the speculation surrounding why Paul had died. "My employees didn't know until it came out in the paper. And later on, when the other shelter employee, Craig, died, Bonnie didn't know about it ahead of anyone else. I don't think she's tapped into an underground gossip society that gives her the info first."

Mark's shoulders slumped like all the evidence against Bonnie was piling up on top of them. "If Al Cahoon had killed Paul, he would have taken the Great Dane puppy with him at the same time."

Why he hadn't taken the Dane puppy was the question that we'd been stumbling over since we figured out she played some part in this. We couldn't answer it because we were asking the wrong question. Paul's killer didn't take the puppy because she didn't care about the Dane puppy at all.

"Cahoon likely would have shot Paul as well. The syringe was more a weapon of opportunity." Mark had his elbows up on the table now like he wanted to lay his head down. "But why would Bonnie kill Paul?"

I turned my back to Mark, unable to bear the look on his face. Hurting him seemed to be what I was best at. "I think it has to do with Toby."

"We don't have proof," Mark said.

We didn't have proof. She'd have to confess to the crime. "I wish I could walk away from this one and leave it unsolved."

But if I did that, I'd be no better than my father, who spent his life helping murderers go free. The truth and the law either mattered or they didn't. I couldn't pick and choose when they did. Look what happened when I thought I should let Craig get away with what he was doing because it sounded like a good thing.

Maybe the best thing for me to do would be to help Bonnie get the shortest sentence possible. The police had nothing on her. As terrible a criminal defense attorney as I'd been, I'd been an equally good negotiator. As long as we didn't go to court, I had a decent chance of helping her.

I turned back around and Mark looked up at me, his face drawn. "What do we do?" he asked.

"I still have my license. I need to talk to her alone."

He looked confused for a second, then his expression cleared. "Because if she says anything to me, I could be asked to testify against her, but her lawyer couldn't."

I nodded.

The door to the kitchen swung open, and Bonnie stuck her head in.

"We've matched all the dogs we can." The brightness of her grin burned my heart. "Do you want them left on the coffee table?"

Mark got to his feet. "How about I paperclip each match together?"

The cheerfulness in his voice sounded forced to me, but maybe I was the only one who would notice, like how grape soda tastes like grape right up until the moment you drink grape juice.

He managed to maneuver Bonnie around so that he stood next to the door and she stood next to me. "Will you stay with Nicole? I'll see everyone out for you."

"Oh, of course." She did her bird-flap flutter with her hands. "We wouldn't want her alone if she's feeling poorly."

Mark slipped out the door, and I licked my lips.

If I was wrong, I was going to lose her as my friend anyway. No one would want a friend who thought them capable of murder. Just like Mark didn't want a friend who thought him capable of adultery.

"Before I came to Fair Haven, I worked as a defense lawyer." My voice cracked and I swallowed. "I need to ask you something about Paul's death, but first I want to offer to be your lawyer."

Bonnie's lower lip did this in-out thing like it was trying to pout and quiver at the same time. My last mental wall standing in her defense crumbled. Her guilt was emblazoned across her face.

"Being my lawyer means you can't share what I tell you with anyone, right?" she said. "Not even the police."

I took her hand and led her to the table. "Not even the police. Not unless you tell me I can."

"I'd like you to be my lawyer." She slumped into her chair and held my hand in an embrace as tight as her hugs. "I didn't do it on purpose. You have to know that. I didn't go there meaning to hurt him. One minute we were arguing about why he wasn't doing more to find the missing dogs, then he ordered me to leave and turned his back on me. The next thing I knew, the syringe was in his neck. I didn't even know what was in it for sure."

I patted her hand. My parents would have lectured me about professionalism and emotional distance, but Bonnie wasn't a normal client. I wasn't even getting paid. "We'll make sure to tell the police that. It means it wasn't premeditated. At worst, you'll get second-degree murder."

"What?" Bonnie yanked her hand away. Her lips firmed into a hard line. "You said you couldn't tell the police anything."

It was the same mixed-emotion push-pull I'd seen in her when Craig insulted her. Except this time she clearly felt safe enough and confident enough to defend herself. I was her friend, after all, not someone who wanted to tear her down.

"I did a good thing." She punctuated the words with a slap of her palm on the table. "You think I didn't see the kinds of missing pets he was ignoring? I *saw*." She snarled the word. "And then he tells me to mind my own? No. We needed someone else managing the shelter who'd care about all the animals equally."

Sometimes I hated myself for seeing people's pressure points and knowing how to push them. I knew now how to get her to agree to confess. I got up, walked over to the door to the living room, and held it open. Thankfully, Mark had made himself scarce.

I pointed to the pictures lying on the table, many of them now matched up with *missing pet* flyers. "I'm not the one who's responsible to saving those dogs. Paul wanted you to leave it alone because he was investigating the dogfighting ring. He needed to keep it quiet until he found enough evidence to stop them."

I might have fudged a little about why Paul wanted Bonnie to stop coming around the shelter. It might have been that she was simply making a pest of herself. But I decided to assume the best of a man who had proven his motives were good.

At the very least, I was going to present the best of him to Bonnie because she'd killed a good man.

Bonnie's hands flittered up from the table and back down again.

And then, before I knew it was coming, she burst into tears. "Who's going to take care of Toby if I go to jail?"

Chapter 26

Heavy snoring woke me with a jolt. I tossed a pillow off the bed in the general direction of the noise. The drone skipped a beat, then took up again louder than before.

I groaned and rolled to the side of the bed. Toby lay flat out on his side on his dog bed, his head tilted back at an angle that looked the opposite of comfortable. The first night he'd been with me, I'd tried to leave him in the laundry room, but he'd whined all night. When I asked Bonnie about it, she told me he'd never slept alone, and so of course he'd cry.

Promising to take Toby had ended up being the only way I could convince her to confess to Paul's murder. Because she'd killed him in the heat of the moment, and because she hadn't intended to kill him when she struck him with the syringe, I'd been able to get her voluntary manslaughter.

I stuck my feet into my fluffy purple slippers, pulled on my robe, and turned off the alarm that hadn't had a chance to sound. I wasn't getting back to sleep with the heavy snoring. Did they make CPAP machines for dogs? I'd swear he had sleep apnea with the way he sounded.

A board creaked beneath my feet. Toby snorted and lifted his jowly head. His tail flopped and he lumbered to his feet.

"Now you decide to get up?"

He cocked his head to one side. I don't know if it was the heavy skin over his eyes or whether he had some sense of what had happened to his "mom," but he managed to look mournful.

I scratched him behind the ear. "Come on, bud. I'll get you some breakfast."

He limped behind me. Based on his injuries and behavior after being rescued, the vet said he thought Toby had been used as a bait animal, basically a training toy for the dogs being conditioned to fight. His large size made him durable, but his good nature must have made him difficult to retrain as a fighting animal. As awful as the experience must have been for him, at least he shouldn't have any lingering aggression issues. Not all of the rescued dogs had been as fortunate, physically and emotionally.

As I dished Toby out his breakfast as per Bonnie's specific instructions, my phone vibrated on the counter. I checked the caller ID before answering. Erik.

I slid my finger across the screen. "How's the shoulder?"

"Not healing fast enough."

I still found it funny to hear even-tempered Erik complain, but being confined to desk work wasn't agreeing with him. "You'll be back on active duty soon."

He made a grumbling noise. "I'm glad you're up. I'm headed into work, but I wanted to swing by and drop something off on my way."

I worried my bottom lip with my teeth. All the paperwork for Bonnie had been finalized long ago, and I no longer worked at the shelter since they'd hired three new full-time staff members. Whatever he was bringing, I couldn't guess at.

I glanced down at my pajamas, peeking out from under my robe. They were powder blue and covered in butterflies. Finding anything sexy or even grown-up-looking in fleece was surprisingly hard, and I'd needed a warm set of jammies for moving here. Even though I wasn't looking at Erik as boyfriend material anymore, a girl still needs to have standards.

If I hurried, maybe I could throw on a pair of jeans instead. "How long until you get here?"

"I'm actually already sitting in your driveway."

Blue butterfly pajamas and robe it was.

I shuffled to the front door, Toby at my heels. I cracked open the door, and a gust of cold wind forced its way in. If the groundhog saw his shadow this year, I was going to catch him and eat him. This winter already needed to end.

Erik climbed out of his cruiser and opened the back door. A white-and-black dog jumped out.

He'd brought back my puppy.

I sprinted down the driveway, or at least did as close to a sprint as I could in floppy slippers. She wriggled and tugged at the end of her leash until he finally let her go. I met her a few feet in front of the cruiser and had to kneel down to keep from being bowled over. She drenched my hands and chin with her tongue.

I made a face and wiped the slobber off my skin, but I couldn't wipe away my grin. "I thought you said I couldn't have her because the law said she had to be adopted out of state."

"Mark found a loophole. Because she was technically stolen, she could be returned to her owners and then they could give her to you."

My throat closed. How was it that even now, when it'd been weeks since we'd seen each other or spoken, Mark still found ways to be on my side? "Mark found a loophole?"

Erik rubbed at his shoulder, and I couldn't help wondering if the cold would always bother him now. It seemed everyone involved had come out with some sort of scar. "He insisted I bring her back to you rather than bringing her himself. He wouldn't explain why. Even suggested I should take the credit for it."

His tone carried a strong vibe of *Would you care to explain?*

I wouldn't. He was a smart man. He could put the pieces together if he tried. "But, of course, that would have been a lie of omission, and I know how you feel about those."

His lips twitched in that almost-but-not-quite-a-smile way of his. "Indeed."

Toby had picked his way down the driveway behind me. I stiffened. What if he and my puppy didn't get along? They'd both been in a situation where they could easily fear or dislike other dogs.

They sniffed each other cautiously, and then my puppy lowered her front, stuck her hindquarters in the air, and barked in a way that clearly said *Play with me!*

Erik touched the brim of his hat with his fingers. "Have a good day, Ms. Fitzhenry-Dawes."

"Same to you, Officer Higgins."

"That's still Interim Chief Higgins. At least for a few more weeks." He opened his cruiser door. "And for what it's worth, I think you should call Mark and thank him."

He closed the door and backed the car out of my driveway before I could figure out a response.

I wasn't going to call Mark. Not ever. Because it was official. The moment I heard he'd been working to find a way to return my puppy to me, I knew I was in love with a married man.

Bonnie's Maple Syrup Cookies

INGREDIENTS:

1 cup softened unsalted butter
1 cup packed brown sugar
1 egg
1 cup maple syrup
1 teaspoon vanilla extract
4 cups all-purpose flour
2 teaspoons baking soda
1/2 teaspoon salt
1/3 cup white sugar

INSTRUCTIONS:

1. Preheat the oven to 375 degrees F (190 degrees C).

2. Spray your cookie sheets with non-stick cooking spray.

3. In a large bowl, cream butter and brown sugar. (To cream butter and sugar, you beat them together using a mixer until smooth.)

4. Add egg, maple syrup, and vanilla. Beat until well blended.

5. Sift together flour, baking soda, and salt. (If you don't have a sifter, you can mix them with a whisk.)

6. Add the flour mixture to the wet ingredients and stir until well blended.

7. Shape the dough into 1-inch balls and roll them in the white sugar.

8. Place the balls onto a cookie sheet. Leave about 2 inches between them. Flatten them with the palm of your hand.

9. Bake 8-10 minutes. Remove to a wire rack and let cool.

MAKES approximately 60 cookies.

LETTER FROM THE AUTHOR

I'm so thankful and excited that you continued on with Nicole's journey alongside me. In the next book, I plan to reveal the truth about Mark's wife. I know many of you have been waiting for it.

If you'd like to know as soon Book 3 (*Almost Sleighed*) releases, sign up for my newsletter at www.smarturl.it/emilyjames.

I'm also putting together a Pre-Release Reader Team. If you join, you'll receive an ebook copy of each book before it's available for purchase. All I ask in return is that you leave an honest review for that book within a week of its release. To join the team, simply send me an email at authoremilyjames@gmail.com.

If you enjoyed *Bushwhacked*, I'd really appreciate it if you also took a minute to write a quick review wherever you bought the book. Reviews help me sell more books (which allows me to keep writing them), and they also help fellow readers know if this is a book they might enjoy.

ABOUT THE AUTHOR

Emily James grew up watching TV shows like *Matlock*, *Monk*, and *Murder She Wrote*. (It's pure coincidence that they all begin with an **M**.) It was no surprise to anyone when she turned into a mystery writer.

She loves cats, dogs, and coffee. Lots and lots of coffee...lots and lots of cats, too. Seriously, there's hardly room in the bed for her husband. While they only have one dog, she's a Great Dane, so she should count as at least two.

If you'd like to know as soon as Emily's next mystery releases, please join her newsletter list at www.smarturl.it/emilyjames.

She also loves hearing from readers. You can email her through her website (www.authoremilyjames.com) or find her on Facebook (www.facebook.com/authoremilyjames/).